Edited by Matthew A. Clarke

Proofread by Nick Clements

This book is dedicated to everyone I ever met or glimpsed from the shadows in the wilderness. More specifically Kingston, Max, Adrian, Tio, The Bangers, Casey and The Dear Hunter, the staff at Aku Aku Tiki Bar in Orlando, Florida, and of course, Shailah.

THE SECRET SEX LIVES OF GHOSTS

Dustin Reade

Planet Bizarro Press

CHAPTER ONE

The woman with the bloody face hangs on to my windshield wipers as I take a sharp right turn at 75 miles per hour. Her pink bathrobe flaps in the wind, and bugs slam into the back of her head as she shouts at me, telling me the names of her children and where they live. As if I care. As if I didn't already know.

I bring it down around 55 mph for a few minutes, letting her think I am bringing us to a stop before flooring it again. I veer to the left and enter a skinny back alley.

"Please," Bloody Lady begs through broken teeth. "They think it was a suicide. If you'll just go to my son's house and dig up the gloves in the flower pot, then my daughter can get the insurance money!"

"Sorry," I say as I tighten my grip on the steering wheel. "Ain't nobody got time for that."

I put the pedal to the metal, and we fly down the alley, knocking over trashcans and scaring the living shit out of mangled-eared alley cats. My tires squeal, straining almost to bursting as I swing around another tight right. The woman says something, pleading with me, but I can't hear her over the roar of the engine, the adrenaline pulsing through my veins.

Suddenly, I slam on the brakes, skidding to an almost immediate halt, flinging the bathrobe'd woman from the hood. Her brain explodes out of her eye sockets as she makes contact with the dead-end wall. She starts to fade away, doing that weird, dust-crumble thing they do, but I am already backing out, heading to the warmth and safety of my office.

The next day, the chubby kid is back. Early twenties, baby-face, ugly as sin with nervous eyes barely contained by his coke-bottle glasses standing in front of my desk, working the brim of his hat in his nervous fingers. I glare at him for a long time, waiting for him to say the first word. I can tell he is uncomfortable, doesn't want to ask but has to, eventually.

Finally, he throws a fake cough into his hand and says, "So, uh...how did it go? Did you find her?"

Lighting a cigarette, I say, "Yeah, kid. I found her."

He swallows a softball-size lump of shame before continuing.

"Did you," he asks. "Did you, uh, I mean, did everything...go alright?"

"You asked me to do a job," I say, blowing smoke in his face. "I did it."

"You mean it?" The kid says, suddenly beaming. "You really killed her?"

"No," I say. "*You* killed her, kid. I just got rid of her ghost for you."

The kid jumps up to shake my hand, singing my praises like a choirboy. I put a stop to that with one hand in his face like a wall. He stares at my palm, confused.

"My fee," I say.

"Oh, yeah!" he says, reaching in his jacket and pulling a money-fat envelope from his inside pocket, "Of course!"

2

He tosses the envelope on my desk, and I open it up and count it real slow with my feet up.

The kid stands there for a few minutes, unsure of what to do next. I take pity on him.

"I trust you can see yourself out?"

"Of course," he says again, gathering his things.

Halfway out the door, he turns around and says, "You really did it? You really got rid of her?"

"You can check the alley behind Kung Pow Chicken and Laundry," I tell him, not looking up from the stack of hundreds. "There might still be some ectoplasm hanging around."

The kid nods, the gravity of what he's done finally evident on his baby-face, lining it with enough self-loathing to age him ten years and eventually shuffle him into adulthood.

CHAPTER TWO

Ten years ago, I put my little sister in the microwave.

We had never really been close.

My parents divorced when I was sixteen. I was an only child, and it tore my world apart when my father moved away and left me with my mother. Not that I would've rather lived with him or anything. To be honest, I think I would have resented whichever parent I ended up with, turning the other into some kind of superhuman while torturing and manipulating the one that got to keep me with guilt.

That's what I did to my mother, anyway.

I stayed out late, brought girls home, and took drugs. I did it right in front of her, shamelessly. Whenever she tried to discipline me, I would scream at her that I was going to live with my father, and she would never see me again if she didn't let me do whatever the hell I wanted.

It hurt her, probably did serious emotional damage, but I didn't care. I think I was genuinely upset about the divorce on a much deeper level than I let on at the time. My father wasn't perfect. Shit, he wasn't even very fun

4

to be around. But I really did miss him, then. Seeing him on the weekends was fine and all, but I missed having him around to fart at the dinner table, or tell me dirty jokes when we were alone in the car together.

So, while the divorce caused an almost irreparable shift in my relationship with my mother, it actually helped to bring my father and me closer together.

...until he remarried.

Stephanie *shudder*. Stephanie the Stepmother was a wicked bitch straight out of a fairy tale. Strictly religious, overbearing, and mean-spirited, we took an instant dislike to one another.

Rather than deal with going to her weirdo-flop-around-on-the-floor-babbling church every Sunday, I started staying at my mother's house more. It actually helped to mend our relationship somewhat, but I still did more or less whatever I wanted, and she still felt powerless to stop me. Then Stephanie got pregnant.

"Son," My father said, standing behind Stephanie with his hands protectively over her shoulders. "We've got something to tell you."

"We're pregnant," Stephanie blurted out, raising one eyebrow cockily as she stared me deep in the eyes. I knew what the look meant; she'd won. She wasn't going anywhere, and I was stuck with her whether I liked it or not.

I most decidedly did not.

Nine months later, Sophia was born. A beautiful baby girl with thick, dark hair and a piercing cry that made you feel like the tiny bones in your ears had shattered and were busily tearing their way out of your head via your eyes.

"She's colicky," Stephanie said. So my father went out and bought every baby-calming stomach medicine he could find. Organic tablets that dissolved in water worked best, but Stephanie demanded they weren't real medicine, and he had to go out and find something stronger. He came back with still more products, none of which worked. But still, Stephanie refused to allow the organic tablets.

Sophia cried constantly. Nothing would soothe her. All the non-organic tablets in the world did no good. It drove us crazy. We lost sleep, and Stephanie and My relationship became even more strained and unpleasant. We would often lash out at each other over the most trivial trespasses. Spilled milk became grounds for screaming matches that lasted for hours. Finally, my father had had enough. He said he was taking the baby to a specialist the next town over, and I was to go with him because he didn't want Stephanie and me to kill each other while they were gone.

"Fine by me," I said.

The next day, we loaded in the car and headed to the hospital. Sophia had been on a roll the night before, screaming nonstop until the sun came up, and it was time to go. We were tired and irritable, shrouded in that strange haze that comes with sleeplessness. I guess that's why my father missed the stop sign.

The truck hit us on the back passenger side, caving in the door and sending us into a wild spin which slammed us into two other vehicles in the opposite lane. I remember a strange, grinding sound and the taste of blood before we slammed into the concrete embankment, and I died.

CHAPTER THREE

Heaven was beautiful. Exactly as I always pictured it: fluffy white clouds, Angels flying around playing harps, dead people playing table tennis with halos over their heads, everything.

Of course, I saw all of this through the gates.

Where I had materialized was more of a celestial waiting room. Saint Peter sat behind a tall desk beside the pearly gates of heaven. He slowly lifted his big, bald head when he saw me.

"Name?"

"Thomas Johansson," I said.

He pulled a big book from some hidden drawer and began scouring the pages with a gnarled finger. That's when I took a quick look through the gates and saw all that stuff I just mentioned.

I was standing there, Saint Peter searching the big book for my name, clucking his tongue, saying, "Nope, sorry, I don't see you anywhere. Are you sure you got the name right?"

"Yes," I said. "Thomas Johansson. I was in a car wreck."

He ran his finger down the page again.

"Sorry," he said again. "I don't see you anywhere. Heaven or Hell, there is nothing. I've got a *Sophia* Johansson, but no Thomas."

I stood there for a moment, not sure what to do. Clearly, I was dead, yet they apparently had no record of me. One has to imagine God keeps his files pretty well in order, so I had to assume the error was not theirs, but what had I done?

"What does that mean?" I asked, finally.

Saint Peter puffed up his cheeks and held out his hands.

"It means you're not dead, kid," he said with an exaggerated exhale. "Congratulations."

He then pulled a lever, and a little trapdoor opened up, dropping me out of the sky. I was thousands of feet up, at airplane altitude, and falling fast. Buildings loomed before me, growing like time-lapse mushrooms as I descended. *Well*, I thought, *if I wasn't dead, then I'm sure as hell about to be*.

A big hand came out of the sky and grabbed me. It pulled me up towards the clouds again, and Saint Peter's face pushed through the clouds, as big as a mountain.

"I almost forgot," he said. "If you see your sister, tell her to get her ass up here. We don't like ghosts running around down there, causing all kinds of existential problems. Ain't nobody got time for that."

"She's just a baby," I told him. "She can't talk yet."

"So what?"

"So," I said, "how am I supposed to make her come up here if I can't tell her anything?"

"Oh, that's easy," he said. "You have to kill her. Ghosts don't know they're dead. You have to make them realize it. But remember, it has to hurt. They have to know there is no other outcome than death. None of that 'slim chance of survival' crap. Now get to it."

With that, he dropped me, and I fell like a brick into my body.

CHAPTER FOUR

It took me months to learn to walk again. As the truck slammed into us, the back door caved in, the metal becoming a jagged point that managed to sever some of the nerves in my back. The doctor said I would never walk again, but of course, I defied all expectations and walked six months later. I was really proud of myself, until my doctor told me he says that to everyone—even people with pneumonia—and it was really more of a joke more than a prognosis.

"Considering you had a genuine back injury," he said, "It may have been in poor taste. I see that now."

All the while, my dead baby sister was screaming and crying in the abandoned nursery. Her wails were loud enough to pierce the ether and seep into reality, giving Stephanie and my father horrible nightmares. I didn't have nightmares, but I couldn't sleep, either. For some reason, after coming back from Heaven, I could see dead people. That sounds cool until you realize dead people are *everywhere*. Seriously, we are never alone. They are always there, reading over our shoulders, touching themselves while looking down our shirts on the bus, rummaging through our shit.

But besides being annoying, they didn't really bother me or anything. They were just sort of *there*. Sophia, though, was becoming more of a problem every day. The cries got louder, and my father started carrying her blankets around the house, singing to them, trying to calm the ghostly wails pouring through the walls. Stephanie turned the Bitch Factor up to eleven. Something had to be done.

So, not knowing what else to do, I walked into the nursery and gathered her ghost up in my arms.

She was surprisingly heavy, like a really fat cabbage made of air. She whimpered as I held her. She sniffled and cried as I carried her down the stairs and into the kitchen, and she screamed as I put her in the microwave. I hit the setting for "Popcorn" and stood back.

She turned in slow, screaming circles, looking disturbingly like a raw chicken. Two minutes went by before she started bubbling. It looked like she had marbles rolling around under her skin. Then her stomach puffed up, and she exploded.

It happened so fast I almost didn't realize it had happened at all. One minute, I was watching her skin boil, and the next, she was gone, replaced with a thick, red sauce that coated the microwave door. My father came in a few minutes later.

"Hey, Son," he said.

"Hey, Dad," I said. "How're you holding up?"

He slowly poured himself a cup of coffee, rolling my question around in his head.

"You know," he said. "It's funny, but I think I actually feel a bit better today. I mean, it's weird, but I suddenly feel like maybe there's hope. I don't know if I'll ever forgive myself for what happened to you two that day, but I think I am coming to accept it a bit more. Does that make any sense at all?"

"It makes perfect sense, Dad," I told him.

He took a drink of coffee and made a face.

"Oh man," he said. "There's nothing worse than cold coffee!"

He opened the microwave, and I left the room before I saw too much.

CHapter Five

A few years later, I was working at this seedy hotel downtown. Rumor had it that Ted Bundy had killed a prostitute in room 308, and the manager was always telling us not to put anyone in that room.

"They always complain," he told me. "No matter who it is, they complain. I have to move them to a different room, or worse, give them a refund. So, save yourself the headache, and just don't put anyone in that room."

So, I didn't put anyone in that room for a while.

I was saving myself the headache.

One night a car pulled up, and these three Rabbis stepped out. They were just passing through, and they wanted a room for the night. We were booked solid, but I didn't feel right sending them back out into the cold. So, I did the only thing I could do: I put them in 308. About three hours later, I got the first call.

"*Oi*, I think there might be trouble," the Rabbi said. "The lady next door is screaming, and I hear thumps. I do! Loud ones! Maybe you should make a call and send in the police or what have you!"

13

"I'll look into it, sir," I told him.

Hanging up, I walked down the hall to 309 and knocked on the door. A young woman answered. Her eyes were red-rimmed with sleep, wrapped up snug in a white bathrobe.

"Sorry to bother you, ma'am," I said. "But we've received a complaint about noise coming from this room. Someone said they heard screaming."

The young woman shook her head slowly, squinting her eyes in confusion.

"I haven't heard anything," she said. "I mean, I fell asleep with the TV on, but I kept the sound down. It's still on now. Does it sound too loud to you?"

I stuck my head in the door. No. The TV was barely audible at all. So I apologized and went back to the office.

Twenty minutes later, the Rabbis called again. This time they said their TV was on the fritz, and all they could get was some weird Closed Circuit feed of a dead body.

"It's horrible, it is!" the Rabbi told me.

I went to check it out, finding the Rabbis in quite a state when I arrived.

Sure enough, the TV was broken. A flickering image of a dead woman stripped of her clothing, blood everywhere, the cheesy artwork on the walls proving beyond a shadow of a doubt that the image had been filmed right there in that room. Then, I heard the screaming. It was coming from the bathroom. I knew what I had to do.

Turning to the gathered Rabbis, I said with a smile, "We apologize for the inconvenience, gentlemen. But if you could all just wait in the office, I believe I can have this all sorted out in a few minutes."

They agreed and walked down the hall to the office while I looked around for some kind of weapon.

There wasn't much. The hangers were all those crappy kinds that are connected to the closet beam (you would not believe how many people try to steal hangers!). The Rabbis hadn't unpacked their bags yet, so I couldn't rummage through their stuff in the hopes of finding a menorah or something with which to bludgeon. Finally, I settled on the red leather Gideon's Bible I found in the dresser drawer.

You know what I always found weird about those things?

We didn't put them in the rooms.

The hotel staff, the management, the housekeepers, we all had nothing to do with those things getting in the rooms. So how did they get there? I imagine some strange creature, like a self-replicating sea jelly shaping itself into a bible and crawling into the hotel through cracks in the foundation, oozing out of the electrical sockets, and laying eggs in the empty dresser drawers.

Anyway, I walked into the bathroom, and there she was, the dead prostitute. She was hiding behind the shower curtain, screaming and holding her hands out as though fighting off an invisible attacker. I raised the bible over my head and brought it down on the bridge of her nose.

Her screams turned into startled gurgles. She lashed out defensively, scratching at my arms with her long, red nails. I brought the book down again and again, cleaving at her face with its corners until her skull gave out, and the book tore through the thin membrane of flesh and made soup of her brains. Then I took a few minutes to pull her apart and flush her body down the toilet, piece by piece. Ghosts aren't like you and me. Their skin is spongy and stretchy, like taffy that's been soaking a puddle.

When I had flushed the last of her face away, I washed my hands and walked back to the office.

"That should do it," I told the Rabbis.

They thanked me and went back to the room. They slept peacefully, and from that moment on, we could check people into 308.

A few days later, my boss took me aside.

"How'd you do it?" he asked. "How'd you get rid of the hooker?"

"I don't know what you mean," I said.

"Don't play dumb with me, kid," he said. "I know you can see 'em too. Now, level with me. How'd you do it?"

I wasn't sure how to answer him. I was worried if I said too much, it would turn out we weren't talking about the same thing and he would think I was crazy. On the other hand, if I continued playing dumb, he might fire me. He was kind of an asshole.

"I read the bible to her," I said, finally. "That's all it took. Most of the time, they just need a little push to let them know it's time to move on."

"The bible," he laughed shrewdly, "sure."

He grabbed me gently by the neck and pulled me in closer so I could smell the coffee and cigarettes on his breath and see the brown and gray hairs on his chest winding through his ostentatious gold necklace.

"Hey, look," he said. "I don't care how you did it, but I need you to do it again. I've got a job for you, if you're interested."

"What kind of job?" I asked.

"The kind that pays five hundred dollars," he answered. He pulled his cell phone out of his pocket and started punching numbers. "I'm going to text you my address," he said. "Tonight, when your shift is over, I want you to come over. It's for dinner, but it ain't *just* for dinner. You understand?"

"I understand," I said.

"Then we understand each other," he said with a sniveling laugh that sounded like an anthropomorphic rat.

I pulled away as gracefully as I could, trying to put the front desk between us, when he called after me. I turned to look. He was standing halfway out the glass door of the lobby.

"A friendly reminder," he said. "Don't forget your bible."

CHAPTER SIX

My boss lived by the quarry. They didn't put street lights in that part of town back then, so the walk was dark and wet. Overhanging branches dripped sludgy rainwater, the murky, brown stuff that gets sponged up in the moss and drips out two or three days after the real rain has dried up everywhere else.

Halfway to his house, a naked man in thick-rimmed glasses emerged from the bushes.

"Hey, man," he said. "Can you see me?"

"Yeah," I said.

"Well, then take a look at *this*!" he reached down, tore his penis off, and flung it at my face. I leaped away from it just in time, and it went flying over my shoulder, landing in the street behind me. The naked guy was already running off up the road.

"Fuck you, man!" I screamed, picking up the spongy ghost penis and throwing it as hard as I could, har-rumphing happily as it whacked him in the back of the head.

Sometimes, the dead can be real assholes.

"Thomas!" My boss said as he opened the door. "Glad you could fuckin' make it! Come in, hey! Did you have any trouble finding the place?"

"No, sir," I said as he took my jacket and hung it on a rack by the door.

"Hey," he said, running his fingers over the collar. "What is 'dis, water? Is it raining or something?"

"It's from the trees," I said.

He nodded like he understood.

"Fuckin' trees," he said. "Hey, forget about the fuckin' trees, okay? Come on inside and get warmed up. *MA!*"

"WHAT?" a screeching voice fell from upstairs.

"MY FUCKIN' FRIEND IS HERE! COME DOWN AND SAY HELLO!"

He led me into the living room, and we waited while someone of apparently sizable girth struggled their way down the stairs. Figuring it would take a while, I took a look around the place.

The entire house had been held in a sort of stasis since the 1970s. Plastic covered the sofas. Dusty pictures of outdated hairstyles in flaking gold frames, an orange carpet that may have been shag, once upon a time, but now it was a flattened, matted canvas of dog hair and cigarette ashes. My boss put a record on the turntable—Martin Denny's *Quiet Village*—and sat across from me on a white and gold loveseat. He was wearing dull yellow pants and a butterfly collar shirt with actual butterflies on it. Glitzy gold rings sparkled on every finger, and his chest hair slowly devoured a thin, gold chain around his neck. He had slicked his wiry hair back, making the few remaining patches of black seem wet, while the grey patches looked like steel wool. He was smiling.

"Hey, uh," he said, leaning forward and whispering conspiratorially. "When my fuckin' ma gets down

19

here, don't say anything about her face, alright? She's, uh...she's got a sort of problem."

"Sure," I said, shaking my head. "No problem. I would never say anything about something like that. What is it, like a birth mark or something?"

"Not exactly," he said, moving his hands in a circle in front of him, searching for the words. "It's more of, like a horrible wound, y'know? But don't look at it or nothing'. I'm just warning you, is all. It's pretty bad."

"Okay," I said. "No problem, I won't look."

"Hey," he held up a ring-covered hand, "I'm serious. When you see this shit, you're gonna be like, *'what the fuck is this shit?'* all right? It's fuckin' disgusting."

Then, he said, "so just be cool."

"Okay," I said as his mother rounded the corner and entered the den.

I wasn't cool.

I wasn't fucking cool at all.

Half of her face was missing. One bloodshot eye on the left side peeked out at the world through heavy eyelids and bags that drooped almost to her nose, which was torn in half at the top, with the right nostril flapping through empty space. Her matted, stringy hair hung in the ice cream scoop-shaped hole on the right side of her face, exposing a hollow bowl of gore. Her mouth remained intact, allowing a constant stream of gargles and wheezes to escape.

This is to say nothing of the rest of her, which took up about as much space in the living room as a medium-sized elephant might in a box car.

"Jesus *Christ!*!!" I screamed as she entered the living room, "OH MY GOD!"

My boss leaped across the coffee table and held me down as I tried frantically to climb up the back of the sofa and escape through the wide picture windows behind me. He put his hand over my mouth and said,

"*Shhh!* It's okay. Hey, remember I told you about it. You're alright, kid, just calm down."

It took me a while, but finally, I was able to calm down enough to choke out a sort of horrified greeting.

"Nice to meet you, ma'am," I gasped. "Sorry about all the screaming. I wasn't quite, uh..."

"WHAT?" the woman screeched.

"She don't hear so good," my boss said. "You gotta really belt it out, but even then it's not the greatest. Hey, you hungry, eh? You want some dinner?"

Meatloaf, a tiny bowl of black olives, and another dish filled with devilled eggs. That was dinner.

I sat in horrified silence, trying not to stare as my boss's mother slurped and grunted her way through her meal. The meatloaf wasn't bad. I stayed away from the finger foods.

"How's the grub?" My boss asked.

"Not bad," I said. Then, for some reason, I said, "thanks."

"Ma, here," he said, indicating his mother with a smile. "She's one of the best cooks in the Tri-County area! Ain't that right, Ma?"

"WHAT?"

"Nothing," He said.

Then, he nodded at me. "You bring your bible?"

I almost choked on a tiny bit of onion.

"Oh, uh," I said. "No, actually, I didn't think I'd need it. I thought we were just going to talk about a job. I didn't think I'd actually be...you know...*doing* anything."

"Jesus, kid, I fucking *told* you to bring your bible!"

"I know," I said. "I'm sorry."

Then, I said, "It doesn't have to be a bible, though. It can be anything."

"I knew it wasn't the fucking bible!" My boss laughed, clapping his hands loudly in the silence of the dining room. His mother didn't seem to notice.

21

"I saw the fucking blood in 308," he said. "I knew you didn't read no fucking psalms!"

He laughed again, sniffing and squinting. *He really does look like a rat*, I thought *like a big Italian rat in a Warner Brothers cartoon*.

"So what do you do," he said, composing himself. "You gotta kill 'em, or what?"

"Something like that," I said. "It's gotta be pretty brutal, though. I mean, they have to really know they're being killed."

"More brutal than a shotgun blast to the fuckin' face?" he asked. He held his hands up. "*Allegedly*," he said. "Allegedly, a shotgun blast to the face."

He seemed lost in thought for a moment, chewing his minuscule cud. Almost to himself, he said, "It's my own fault, really. I chickened out. Shot her from behind while she was watching *Donahue*."

I cleared my throat. It kind of seemed like he had forgot I was there.

"Allegedly," he smiled. "So what d'ya think? Can you help me out with my, uh...Oedipal Complex?"

I took a bite of meatloaf, unsure of what to say.

So I said, "*Sometimes, it's pretty messy*," even though I'd already said that a second ago.

"Hey," my boss said. "Whatever the fuck you gotta do, just get rid of her. You do that for me, and I'll give you five hundred big ones, a'ight?"

"Alright," I said, pushing my seat back and standing up. "You might wanna wait in the living room."

"Oh, sure, sure," he laughed, wiping his mouth with the table cloth and backing away from the table. "Gotta let the artist work, right? Picasso probably didn't let a bunch of gaping motherfuckers watch him while he painted, right?"

"Something like that," I said.

22

I didn't have the heart to tell him Picasso *loved* an audience. He even let filmmaker Henri-Georges Clouzot film him while he created twenty different paintings, drawings, and sketches. It hardly seemed relevant at the time, and I might not have known it then. I'm not sure how I know it now, actually. I mean, I've seen the movie, but it seems weird that I can bring it to mind so readily.

But I digress.

My boss leaned over his bulky sack of dead mother and gave her a gentle kiss on the cheek.

"I'm gonna miss you, Ma," he said. "But, fuck me, you just gotta move the fuck on, you know? Step into the fuckin' light, or whateva."

"*WHAT*?"

"Alright," he said. He gave her one last pat on the shoulder, and looked at me.

"Five hundred bucks," he said.

"Okay," I said.

Once he was out of the room, I closed the doors and started clearing all of the dishes off the table. I stacked them neatly on the floor, and then I removed the tablecloth and busted off one of the table legs. The table was pretty old, so the leg snapped off easily. I propped the legless end up on a chair, and then I started winding the tablecloth around the table leg.

My boss's mother was still eating, completely oblivious to what I was doing. I climbed onto the table and stood over her, my feet on either side of her plate, holding the table leg like a spear. Quick as I could, I kicked her plate away. She looked up at me, stunned, and I brought the table leg down into her mouth, pushing as hard as I could, forcing the leg and cloth down her constricting windpipe, breaking through the soft esophageal lining, rupturing her lungs, and finally bursting through to her stomach. She struggled, clutching at the table leg as it protruded from her gaping mouth. I grabbed her flabby arms and pinned them to the table by standing on her hands as I slowly worked the table leg free, careful to leave the cloth inside her, with only a tiny flap sticking out.

"I'm going to kill you," I told her.

Then I remembered she couldn't hear me (not having an inner ear will do that to a person), so I drug my finger real slow across my neck like a knife, rolling my eyes back into my head and pointing at her. She lunged forward, head-butting me in the crotch and sending me flying across the room.

My back slammed into the far wall, and it took me a second to catch my breath.

My boss's mother clawed at her concave face. She struggled to find the towel end, as it had become dislodged from her top lip and was flapping uselessly in the gaping hole where the right side of her head used to be.

I climbed to my feet and leaped up onto the table, racing over and planting my foot into her chest, knocking her back in her chair. Once again, I stood on her hands and finger-knifed my throat.

It got the point across. She struggled, but I held her firm.

While the fear in her eyes was at its peak, I grabbed the tablecloth and ripped it from her throat-hole. Her organs erupted from her ravaged throat, a spewing volcano of ruptured intestines, blood, and devilled eggs.

She evaporated in minutes, and I went into the kitchen to clean myself up, already thinking about how I was going to spend those five hundred dollars.

CHAPTER SEVEN

"Vinnie the Snitch," the greasy man in the sharkskin suit says as he slides the folder full of pictures across the desk at me. I look through them. A bunch of black and white photos of a skinny guy in flamboyant collared shirts and huge sunglasses that make him look like some kind of insect.

Like, a grasshopper, or something.

Maybe an ant.

"Little bastard has been making trouble ever since we whacked him last summer," Sharkskin tells me. "He's been knocking shit over, touchin' himself in the bathroom, and all that. Little pervert is ruining the business! Now, officially, the boss don't really know for sure that it's Vinnie, on account of he ain't a psychic like you or whatever, but he says, 'if it's him, then we should know about it, right?'"

"Sounds like a wise man," I say, still looking at the pictures.

"Vinnie? Naw, he was a pervert, always jerkin' his off switch. It was disgustin', it really was."

"No," I say. "I meant your boss."

"My boss ain't never yanked it in front of nobody," Sharksin says.

"Listen," I tell him, "how about we just forget it?"

The thing about the picture: I recognize the guy. I had seen him a few years ago. He was the naked guy that chucked his penis at me on my way to kill my boss's mom. I look at Sharkskin again. Everything about this guy screams MAFIA, but business has been slow lately, and I could use the extra scratch.

All this is happening now, right now, way after all that flashback stuff.

I let my eyes move over my office and its meager furnishings, and suddenly it dawns on me that we both look like stereotypes. Sharkskin with his suit and grease and meaty knuckles, and me with my fedora, my vest over the white button-up, the sleeves rolled up to the elbows. The desk. The cigarette smoking in the ashtray. The door with my name on it. My hangover.

It all helps to paint a ridiculous picture straight out of a Mickey Spillane novel.

Or is it Nicky?

Nicky Spillane doesn't sound right to me. It doesn't sound tough enough.

"Anyway, so that's why I gotta bring you in," Sharkskin says, making a face like, *you gotta do what you gotta do.*

Or maybe it means, *nothing personal. It's just business.*

Or something.

"Okay," I say, standing up. "Take me to your leader."

CHAPTER EIGHT

On our way to the restaurant, Sharkskin leans over and taps me on the shoulder. We are riding in the back of a sleek, black limo. The backseat looks like a red velvet cake with white frosting on the seams.

"So, these dead guys," he asks me, "do you see 'em all the time, like walkin' around and shit, all mixed in with people, or is it something you can turn on and off?"

Looking out the window at the rows and rows of head wounds, nooses as neckties, flattened animals darting between legs, I shake my head.

"All the time," I sigh. "All the time."

CHAPTER NINE

Fish everywhere, its smell gets in my clothes, in my eyes. A rotten, oceanic smell that is somehow dusty and wet simultaneously. I imagine long, tuberous fish swimming in a thin layer of sand. I picture them leaping out of the tips of sand dunes like dolphins, the sand splashing around them as they crash back down.

"Fish never get chapped lips," I say.

"What?" Sharkskin asks as he leads me through the rows of tables and chairs of the empty restaurant, past the bar with its hanging glasses, into the wide, swinging doors of the kitchen with their two circular windows near the top, covered in steam.

"Nothing," I say, my shoes catching on the grimy linoleum. "I was just talking to myself. I do that sometimes. It's sort of a hazard of the trade."

"Hmph."

I suppose I could have told him I was talking to a dead person, but whatever. I don't really care if he thinks I'm crazy or not. That's not my problem. The fact is fish *can't* get chapped lips because they don't have lips in the first place! I imagine a fish with big, red kissable lips like in a cartoon. I picture it swimming up to a diver and saying, "Well, *hello*, Sailor!" and then planting a big wet, Bugs Bunny-style kiss right on his facemask.

We keep walking. The kitchen seems to go on forever. At one point, I'm reasonably certain we leave the restaurant and cross an alley, entering another establishment from the backdoor. We pass another long bar, stripper poles and dance music, red lights, and the same rancid fish smell everywhere. I started to get confused. There is no order to the internal layout of this place. Kitchens lead to more kitchens which in turn lead to long hallways that lead to even longer hallways. I feel like we are taking a kitchen-only tour of every restaurant in the world as if somehow they are all connected to one another via back doors and alleyways. I imagine a long, subterranean tunnel running under every business on earth, accessible only to headwaiters and chefs. Something about the thought terrifies me, as if some curtain covering the secrets of reality were being pulled back for an instant, revealing a horrible network of unseen places beneath the world. I shudder, and Sharkskin puts his hand on my back.

We reach another door, lined with gold trim, and Sharkskin pushes it open with a grunt. I think to myself that, surely, this must be the last door.

More kitchens, more tables stacked five-deep with chairs, the legs up in the air like warped pitchforks. In one corner, the ghost of a Japanese businessman sits beside the jukebox, a glass of red wine in his hand. He raises his glass to me. I ignore him.

We reach another set of doors, and Sharkskin tells me, "This is it. Now when we get in there, don't say nothin' stupid or anything, understand? Don't open your mouth unless he asks you a question, you got it? None of this fish business, *capiche*? This is a fish business."

"Gotcha," I say, winking and clucking my tongue at him. He looks at me weirdly for a second, like he suddenly thinks this might be a bad idea, but eventually, he holds the door open, and I walk through.

Another kitchen: Fish everywhere, lining the walls, dripping goo from huge bowls where their ugly faces stare over the rims, packed in ice, lying out on counters drawing flies. An elderly Japanese man in a yellow business shirt and bright green apron is busy hacking into a six-foot sturgeon with a meat cleaver. He slams the cleaver into the chopping block when he sees me, embedding it deep into the hard wood surface.

"Mr. Johansson," he says happily, wiping his hands on the apron and extending one out to me. "It's a pleasure to meet you! I am Antonio Fontana, at your service."

"A pleasure," I say, somewhat awkwardly. "Antonio, huh?"

"That's right," Antonio Fontana says, shaking his very Japanese head courteously. "Is there a problem?"

"No, no," I say, "not at all. It's just, well, with a name like that, I would've thought you'd be, I dunno...more Italian, I guess."

"I get that all the time," Antonio says. He doesn't say it irritated or anything. In fact, he seems to be enjoying this. I decide to push it a bit, see how much I can get away with.

"I must say, though, I can't imagine what The Mob would want with a ghost hunter. I always thought you guys were pretty good at taking care of problematic people."

Antonio Fontana looks hurt and confused by this. He places one hand on his heart and says, "Whatever gave you the impression we were The Mafia?"

"Mafia, Yakuza, whatever," I say casually. "It's all the same thing. Either way, what do you want from me?"

30

See, I am trying to play the tough guy card, act like I don't really care about any of this, but the truth is, I could use the work. I owe money all over town. Not to Bookies or anything like that. Reality is pretty mundane, even for a guy that kills ghosts for a living. My power bill is over a thousand dollars. I keep going in and putting down whatever I can, a hundred here, a hundred there, but I just can't stay on top of the fucking thing. Every time I get it down to a manageable amount, the new bill comes in and pushes it right back into unmanageable numbers. And it's not just Utilities. No. I owe the Library seventy dollars in late fees, and my credit cards are all maxed out. I'm pretty well bent over and fucked. This might be my last shot at keeping a roof over my head and a book on the nightstand. I figure these Mafia Guys might respect me a bit more if I act cool, aloof.

"Hold on," Antonio says, putting his hand up. "First of all, The Mafia and Yakuza couldn't be more different. Secondly, I run a *restaurant*. What part of that makes you think I am a gangster?"

"*This* place?" I ask incredulously, indicating the restaurant. I point to the sturgeon on the table as if it is somehow the most damning piece of evidence in the room. "I mean, no offense, but this has got to be a front, right? Like, you only have the restaurant so you can explain where all the drug money comes from, or whatever."

"Hey!" Sharkskin says, walking over and shoving his finger in my chest. "The boss has been running this place since 1982, when he bought it from my grandfather! They were in the war together, and I'll have you know, this fish," he walks over and lifts the giant fish in one massive, sausagey hand, "is fucking delicious!"

"That's right," Antonio says, wiping his eyes. I had no idea I'd offended him so much. I mean, not to the point of crying anyway. "And it hasn't always been easy. People think because I'm Japanese, I have to make sushi, or rice balls. Well, I bought an *Italian* restaurant. I bought it from one of the finest men I've ever known, and I'll be damned if I am going to change *one item* on that menu to fit your negative stereotypes!"

The two men hug, weeping openly. I feel like a hat made of shit.

"I'm sorry," I say, but they don't hear me.

I step a bit closer and put my hand on Antonio's shoulder. Slowly, he pulls away from Sharkskin and looks at me. He has a long line of brownish snot running down his nose, balancing just over his top lip. I clear my throat.

"I'm sorry," I say. "Sometimes, I'm a little hard on people. It's my work, you see. The things I have to do, the things I see. Well..."

"It makes you hard," Antonio says, nodding. "Yes. Yes, I can see how it might."

"I think we've all learned a few things about stereotyping today," Sharkskin says, and we all nod our agreement like a couple of fucking bobbleheads.

CHAPTER TEN

After I killed my boss's mother, my life changed. It turns out there is a pretty good market for people that see ghosts. That little bastard from *Sixth Sense*[1] could've been pretty rich if he'd tried a little harder.

I started by giving séances, but I had to stop when I was told I wasn't entertaining enough. It wasn't enough that I could send messages to lost loved ones, or ask granddad where he buried the money. No. People wanted a show. John Edwards might look like he's just standing there, but it's all part of the act. The hair, the vacant, loving expression, it's all a finely tuned entertainment mechanism. Plus, he had charisma.

I most emphatically do not.

So I kept working at the hotel for a while, getting jobs on the side from my boss whenever he found me one. I killed Great Aunts, Nephews, Grandparents, stray poltergeists. You name it. But the real money came when I discovered a vein of untapped guilt and ghosts.

"I'm particularly interested in your hospice work," Antonio says, sliding a glass of dark red wine across the table at me. "Tell me a little more about that."

"I don't like to talk about my clients," I say, sipping the wine. It is very gross.

"Of course," Antonio says. "Patient confidentiality is very important in my line of work as well."

"See," I interrupt. "That right there! The way you said that makes it seem like you have something to hide. It sounds exactly like the sort of thing a Mafia Don would say."

"Again with the Mafia shit," Sharkskin says in the corner. Antonio holds up one hand and nods.

"He's right," he says. "That absolutely sounded like something a bad guy would say. What I meant was I understand the nature of business is delicacy, especially if one is in the restaurant business, eh?"

He laughs. Sharkskin laughs too. It takes me a minute to realize that he made a pun. It does not strike me as very funny, so I just sort of smile and say, "Yeah, I guess. Whatever."

"I mean," Antonio says as he wipes laugh-tears from his eyes, "I get why you can't tell me specifics about what you did at Hospice. I wouldn't want to give you my recipes, or tell you where I buy my fish. However," he holds up both hands in front of his face and sort of vogues them in a frame around his head, silently, before continuing, "I would have no problem telling you what *kinds* of things I put in a dish, you understand? After all, if someone orders salmon, it would be foolish to deny there was salmon in the dish, correct?"

"I guess," I say, totally lost.

"So, why don't you tell me, in a roundabout, generic sort of way, the sort of things you did while employed at Hospice Care?"

"I killed ghosts."

Antonio smiles and claps his hands. The answer seems to have satisfied him, even though I didn't tell him anything he didn't already know. Maybe he just wanted me to say it out loud? Seems weird, but who am I to be critical?

Again, who the fuck am I to judge anybody?

My friend Jerry worked for hospice. You know, where old and sick people go to die? It's supposed to "put death back in your hands" or something. Something about the dignity of dying. Something about taking charge. Something about medicating instead of treating, masking pain instead of shrinking tumors. Anyway, it turns out a lot of hospice workers feel guilty for just stepping back and letting everybody die. They feel helpless, useless. More so if they actively helped them make their final exit. Even *more* so if it was one of their own loved ones. They felt haunted, denied the "he's gone to a better place" crap that gets the rest of us through those difficult times. They watched as Grandpa forgot everyone's name, mumbled to himself, and had difficulty chewing shredded chicken. They saw the spirit dissolve before the body gave it up.

If you die slowly, peacefully, it doesn't matter how happy you are, how sure of your final exit.

You're going to stick around.

Bumbling ghosts of wrinkled skin making walls bleed, knocking books off the shelves and so on like a plague. People generally can't see them, but they know something is wrong. Walk through a cemetery, a hospital, a retirement home. You can feel the heaviness of every dead old dude like an elephant skin coat.

So, I killed them again. Forget the gentle exit, sweet-release-of-death stuff they signed up for while they were choking out their last few hours. I bashed in taffy-like skulls, tore limbs apart and used them as

35

bludgeons. I broke bones that no longer existed and slit invisible throats with rusty steak knives.

I was good.

Hospice workers were fucking skipping down the halls when I was done.

Antonio slides a money-fat envelope across the table at me. It is sitting on top of the folder with all the information on the perverted ghost.

When I take the money, he touches my index finger very gently with his pinky and says, "Marvelous."

Later, as I'm led back through the labyrinthine hallways once more, I hold the picture up for the dead Japanese businessman to inspect. Sharkskin watches me from the doorway as I talk to (what looks to him like) an empty chair.

"No, sorry," the Japanese guy says, shaking his head. "I haven't seen him."

"Are you sure?" I ask. "Take a closer look. The owner seems to think he's been causing problems around here."

"Antonio?" the ghost asks. "That guy's a jerk off. Did you know he waited eighteen minutes to call for an ambulance the night I died in here?"

"Maybe so," I say. "But what about this guy?"

He checks the picture again, squinting.

"Are we going or what?" Sharkskin hollers impatiently.

I don't answer him. I just hold up one finger, keeping my eyes on the Japanese ghost.

"Noooo," he says, dragging the word out slowly. "I've never seen that man before in my life." He then elbows me in the ribs, winking and laughing softly.

"Get it?" he asks, "'Never seen him before...*in my life*!'"

"Yeah, I get it," I say, snatching the picture and tucking it into my coat pocket. "You're hilarious."

Sharkskin holds the door open for me as we leave, and I walk right through a naked old lady rubbing her tits on a homeless guy's head while he sleeps.

1. Bruce Willis was dead the whole time.

CHAPTER ELEVEN

Dead people are perverts.

Most of them, anyway.

After my accident, I saw them masturbating their taffy penises at Bus Stations, sniffing women's crotches as they paid for groceries, and worse. You wouldn't believe the shit I've seen. The long, dark pornographic afterlife awaits us is so sexually depraved that it makes the darker corners of the internet look like the Disney Channel.

I asked one of them about it once. An old guy I met in the park. I knew he was dead because his chest was a gaping hole full of frayed innards. He'd spent the better part of the day lying on the benches until women sat on his face.

When I asked him why the dead were so sexual, he told me it was because most of them had spent most of their lives doing things they thought were supposed to get them into heaven after they died: leading good lives, avoiding drugs and alcohol, abstaining from sex, that sort of thing.

"Then it happens, and it's just this same old world over again," he told me. "No heaven, no angels, no rewards for all those carnal impulses denied, so why not get a little pervy? It takes a while to really let yourself get into it. I spent the better part of six years sneaking around college dorms, sniffing underwear, peeking over shower stalls, before it hit home that I could do whatever I wanted."

We sat in silence for a few minutes. I think I might've chewed my lip, or picked some dirt out of my fingernails. Then, I said, "Heaven is real, by the way."

Then, I said, "I've been there."

I don't remember what he said after that because right after he said it, a lady came and sat on his face.

CHAPTER TWELVE

If the quarry at night is a dark, wet place, then the quarry in the daytime may as well be a different country altogether. Dry, dusty, and hot, the street seems like it is perpetually under construction. The air is heavy with the rumble of work trucks, the banging of garbage can lids, and rock music filtering out of the few dilapidated houses. These noises come together to give the entire area the general feeling of a low-rent suburb on the outskirts of Hell.

I have come to this part of town to look for Vinnie the Snitch.

There are two ghosts fighting over a dead pigeon in the middle of the road. They could plainly see me from where I'm standing, but they are too wrapped up in their drama to pay me any mind. Plus, if they do happen to see me, I'll just put my finger up to my lips and shake my head like they do in the movies. The ghosts will nod knowingly, maybe wink or give me a thumbs-up, and go about their business.

I wait under a leafless tree, just sort of standing there, hoping to catch a glimpse of Vinnie the Pervert. The Snitch, I mean. Who cares?

I guess I could have stuck around the restaurant for a while to see if he would come around, but I felt this was as good a place to start as any, seeing as how the last time I saw him, it was here. Dig it?

I see my boss sitting on his front porch a few houses down, talking to a young redheaded girl in overall shorts. Her hair is up in pigtails, and she looks too young to be talking to him, but she is smoking a cigarette, so I have to assume she is at least eighteen. Something about the scene makes me deeply uncomfortable, so I focus on the two ghosts busy beating the hell out of each other in the middle of the street.

Hours pass. The sun seems to be fighting the urge to go down. It hangs in the sky like a huge, sagging testicle, pouring heat down on my head and neck until I think I might die. I'm serious. I am so hot I feel like I could just lay down right here and turn into a shriveled little husk of black shit.

I am about to do just that when I see Vinnie come walking around the corner.

He is naked, casually playing with his flaccid penis while he strolls around, peeking in windows and shouting at the construction workers in the gravel pit. I crouch down in the tree's shade, trying my best to hide as he walks up onto my boss's porch. He says something I can't quite make out, and to my surprise, both my boss *and* the redheaded girl answer back. What the hell does that mean? Can she see ghosts, too? I haven't met too many people that can, so it would be weird if my boss just happened to be hanging out with some runaway-prostitute-whatever that magically had the same incredibly rare ability, wouldn't it?

The two ghosts that had been fighting have stopped and are now just standing there staring at me. Did I say all that out loud? I check my position. I am still relatively hidden from the porch, but if everyone on the porch can see ghosts, they would surely wonder what the hell these two were looking at, and I couldn't let them give away my position.

"Hey," I say, "you guys wanna see something cool?"

They nod excitedly and walk over. Quick as I can, I grab the two of them and slam their heads together. They explode on impact. A fountain of blood erupts from their busted skulls and covers my neck, chest, and head in goop.

I roll the bodies into a tight ball and shove it into my pocket before rechecking the porch.

Everyone is looking at me. Right. Fucking. At me.

"Uh," I say, stepping awkwardly out into the street. "Hiya!"

My boss stands up, squints, puts his hand over his eyes as if that is gonna make this scene make any more sense.

"Thomas?" he asks. "Holy fuckin' shit, is that *you*?" He starts walking down the steps towards me, smiling. His hand is out, ready for a shake, and he keeps it out like that the whole way down the block until he gets to me. Despite the fact that we have both had ample time to prepare for it, I somehow still manage to grab only the ends of his fingers and sort of twitch-shake his skeletal hand.

"Long time no see!" He says happily.

"Yeah," I say, "it's, uh, it's been a while, huh?"

"A while, it's been fuckin' *YEARS*! What are you doin' out here in da Quarry?"

As he talks, he slings his arm around my neck and starts leading me toward the house. I worry that this will blow my whole operation until I remember that Vinnie

42

has no clue I'm there to kill him, so the only way this gets fucked up is if I somehow fuck it up myself.

I am terrified.

The front porch is painted a dull, peeling red, and every single board creaks as I step on it. Vinnie the Pervert leans against the banister, and the redhead remains seated on the dusty porch swing as I approach. Upon closer inspection, I can see she is even younger than I thought, but there is something strange about her face. It ripples occasionally, and I see a much older face beneath. It happens infrequently, and I keep thinking I'm imagining it until I realize I would've had to imagine it about fifty times in the last three minutes, so it's probably really happening. My old boss sticks a finger into the bony part of my chest.

"Moira, Vinnie," he says, "This is Thomas. He used to work for me."

"Ooh," Vinnie says, reaching down and fiddling his rapidly growing erection. "Where've you been hiding?" He gets real close, and I can see the gaps in his teeth. "Are you sure you wanna be outta the business?" he asks. "I'd pay a lot for your Pole Rental."

"Easy, Vinnie," my old boss says, pushing Vinnie gently away. "I didn't mean that. He used to work for the hotel. He's not a Tenement."

Vinnie clucks his tongue disappointedly.

"Shame," he says.

"Yeah, whatever," my old boss says, more or less brushing him off. "Moira, say hello to Thomas. Don't be rude."

"Hello," Moira says. She reaches her hand out with palpable disinterest, and the minute I take it, she becomes an old woman and dies.

43

CHAPTER THIRTEEN

"You feeling any better?" my old boss asks as I sip my Lemon Zinger tea with Honey.

"A little," I say. "Sorry I vomited on your porch. I'll clean it up."

"Don't worry about that. I'm just sorry I didn't warn you a little better. I thought you knew about Body Rental."

"No," I tell him. "It's not your fault. You had no idea I was coming. I should have called first."

"Hey," he says. "Forget about it! I'm glad you dropped by. It's been a long time, and I'm glad to see you. How's your tea? Is it hot enough? I can microwave it for you if you like it a bit hotter. Or maybe I could put an ice cube in it. Lots of people like tea different ways, y'know?"

"I know," I tell him, "the tea is fine. Thank you."

"I like mine with a little milk in it."

"Sometimes," I say, "I like mine that way, too."

He lights a cigarette. We are sitting at the same table we sat at the night I shoved a fucking table leg down his dead mother's throat. Not a lot has changed since

44

the last time I was here. He got a new table cloth, but otherwise, things look exactly the same. We spend a few moments looking at each other. I finish my tea. It is almost boring except for the fact that there are two ghosts and an old dead woman in the other room waiting to see how I'm doing, how I'll react, how I'll deal with the news that there is an underground prostitution ring for the recently deceased and my former employer is one of the leading pimps in the Tri-County Area.

"English style," my boss says.

"Excuse me?"

"That's what they call it in England," he says, "English style. That's when it's just the sugar and milk, I think."

"That sounds right," I say. "In India, I hear they put spices in it, and honey."

The redheaded girl, Moira, walks into the kitchen and sits down opposite us. Through the dull light of the 40-watt, I can see the dingy yellow walls behind her through her pale cheeks. My boss offers her a smoke, she takes one, lights up, and I take one too. I put my hands on the table like I'm holding a tiny, invisible box and say, "So, explain to me how all this works."

How it works is like this: Dead People Wanna Fuck. Pretty much, that's *all* they wanna do. Should be easy, right? I mean, they can go anywhere, almost no one can see them, and it's not like they can get shot or anything, so what's stopping them? Apparently lots of things, the most important being they can't feel anything, so their sexuality is more mental than physical. Like I said before, the skin of a ghost isn't the same as the skin of a living person. It is strangely elastic, cold, and it turns out it's basically totally numb all of the time.

"It's like my tits are asleep," Moira explains at one point, "And my pussy and my arms and legs and face and ass, all asleep."

45

She takes a drag of her cigarette and says, "It fucking sucks."

I don't know what to say, so I don't say anything. I just sit there and sort of nod as the rest of the information gets stored in the back of my brain, and I hope and pray the next time I die, it is forever and permanent and not numb and pervy like it seems to be for other people.

Anyway, to absolutely no one's surprise, *living* people like to fuck, too. We all pretty much just wanna fuck everybody all of the time. It's a fact of life and evolution. However, most people are religious, nervous, or aware of basic rights and freedoms and laws, so they don't really feel comfortable just running around and fucking everyone they see.

The dead, however, suffer from no such compunction.

"So what they do, excuse me, what *we* do," my boss explains, "is we pair up those members of society lookin' to get a little freaky, but who might lack the balls to go out and get a piece, we pair him up with some dead guy out lookin' to grease his numb old boner. The ghost pops in—like possesses him or whatever—fucks a few people, and then it pops out again in time for the John to shower and get back to the family, you get it?"

"Yes," I say. "You paint a very descriptive portrait."

"Tanks," he says, leaning back in his chair and smiling happily.

"But where do you find the people?" I ask.

"Tenements," Moira says.

"Excuse me?"

"We call them Tenements," she says. "You know, like the buildings?"

"Yeah," I say. "Okay, then, where do you find the Tenements?"

My boss laughs hard at the question. Little flecks of spit fly out of his mouth and spray down the table's surface. He laughs until he is coughing so hard he has to lean over and almost vomit onto the floor.

Finally, he sits back and says, "Are you kidding? Are you seriously asking me where we find people looking to fuck somebody? Fucking *everywhere*, we find 'em!"

I look at the redhead. She is staring at me with a look that is either mild curiosity or bored contempt.

"And you do this too?" I ask her. "You rent people or whatever?"

One corner of her mouth lifts, and for a second, I think she is about to smile, but just like that, the look is gone, and she just says, "Sometimes."

"You wanna try it?" my boss asks, leaning over the table and catching me with his rodent-like eyes. "You wanna let one of 'em in you?"

"I don't know," I say. "I mean, sure, it sounds interesting, but...well, does it hurt?"

"Does having sex hurt?" he asks. "Does it hurt when you yank your crank on the can? Hell no, it doesn't hurt. In fact, you won't even know it is happening."

He leans back in his chair and puts his hands together in a tight fist.

"It's like drugs," he says. He blossoms both hands out in front of him like a mini-explosion, or a flower blooming. "Your mind expands."

He shakes his head with a smile and returns to his cigarette.

"It's un-fucking-real," he says.

I look at Moira, try to read her face, but it's like wallpaper or something. I almost wonder if she's even really paying attention, but in all honesty, the idea of her running around inside my body is...well, strangely exciting. I mean, I don't find her sexually attractive as such, but there is definitely something about her that intrigues me. Maybe it's the fact that she is so unreadable? That's probably it: I want to figure her out, see what makes her tic. Though why I want to do this is a question for another time, I think. The point is, I'm interested. And who knows, maybe some of her would rub off on me? Like, maybe I would be able to get a read on her if I let her take the wheel for a while? So, finally, I nod my head and say, "Sure. Let's do it."

"*HOT DOG!*" Vinnie the Pervert screams, racing naked into the room and leaping into the crotch of my jeans.

CHAPTER FOURTEEN

I am standing in front of a farmhouse with peeling paint, windows with black trim and planter boxes, and my massive, decomposing corpse standing like the Statue of Liberty behind it. The house is instantly familiar to me. Without stepping inside, I can see the dusty doilies hung over the backs of ancient armchairs, the dried cicada shell on the kitchen window sill, the footprints carved in the dust coating the stairwell. The air smells of pie and water over dirt. A cornfield grows to my left. A light breeze shuffles through the ears, bouncing the stalks together in an ocean of natural applause. A crop-duster approaches the field from maybe twenty miles off. It's hard to tell distance when it comes to sky-borne objects. I look at the farmhouse again.

Despite having never really left the city, I know this place inside and out. Even the gravel crunching under my converse is familiar. The plane is closer now, and I stand and watch in awe as the bottom butterflies open and releases a thick cloud of heavy, red mist.

The front door opens, and an old woman walks out with a broom. She is dressed in old clothes, worn but clean, obviously handmade. Her hair is pulled back in a tight bun, and the grey hair is shiny where the light hits it. The red mist has spilled over the corn, coating it in a bloody outer layer. The old woman looks at the corn with a disapproving face. The mist starts spilling over the log fence surrounding the corn, approaching us both like a slow flood. The old woman huffs under her breath. I look at her and smile. She waves me over frantically.

"Hurry up and get in the house," she says. "I don't want you breathing in any of that shit."

As Vinnie the Pervert sank into my crotch, I felt blue. By that, I don't mean I felt depressed. I mean I felt like the color blue had saturated my body, starting in my balls and spreading out and over my skin, blooming out from my internal organs and swallowing me whole until I was bluer than the *No Signal* screen on a modern television. I reached out with one hand for...well, anything, I guess.

"Wait," I said.

"Just relax," I heard Moira say.

My vision closed in around me, siphoning down into a pinhole before winking out entirely. There was a massive, internal shift, like my organs had each taken a collective step to the right, and then I found myself in a wide tunnel. The walls were red and wet like the inside of a cyclopean throat. I wasn't walking, but falling, not down but forward, being propelled by unseen hands down the meaty walls of the tunnel toward some unknown destination. The blue sensation had left me, and I could feel every cell of my body stretching to its limits until I lost all outlines and was a free-floating blob of ectoplasm and dreams.

"Just relax," Vinnie the Pervert said in my ear. "I've got you."

The tunnel ended in an abrupt wall of yellow light, and I found myself standing in front of the farmhouse. *I also remember something about driving a car with a rough steering wheel that gave me blisters on my hands.*

As the old woman puts the kettle on, I take a look around the room. It's an antiquated kitchen, with a heavy iron stove and numerous pans and utensils hanging on the wall behind. The old woman wipes her hands on her apron and turns around, smiling.

"Tea," she says. "Doesn't that sound nice? My mother always said, 'no matter how busy life gets, there is always time for a nice cup of tea.'"

"She sounds like a smart woman," I say.

"You're goddamned right she was smart," the old woman says. "She outlived three husbands and fourteen cats, only one of them was a tabby."

From outside, we hear the sound of something enormous slamming into the ground. The whole house shakes with the crash. It sounds like a meteor has slammed into the backyard, and I leap to my feet instantly. The old woman puts up a reassuring hand.

"Don't worry about the noises," she says. "It's just your body collapsing."

"Oh," I say. "Okay."

She sits down in the chair opposite me and puts her hands on the table.

"Listen," she says. "This tea is going to take a while. Water around here isn't the same as other places. Why don't you go on upstairs and change your clothes? I'll get some cookies going. You remember where your room is?"

"I'll figure it out," I tell her before climbing to my feet and walking out of the kitchen.

A hallway with stairs leading up to the second floor separates the kitchen from the living room. Whereas the light and general atmosphere of the kitchen is strangely

51

baby blue, the light from the living room seems brown with yellow undertones. The hallway itself is a dusty white with sepia photographs in heavy frames, and the stairs are thick, old, and brown, shiny with varnish. They creak as I ascend.

Dust particles fill the upstairs as I emerge onto the landing. Doors line the walkway, each paneled, closed, and decorated with ornate handles that seem cold no matter the weather. Somehow, I know which room is mine. I walk to it and try the knob, feel the reassuring weight of it in my hands. It resists for a split second, then cracks open, pushing through the disuse of years and allowing me inside.

A heavy, dust-covered bed: Dust everywhere. Dust rules this world. Dust chokes the engines of the farm equipment outside. Dust colors our hair—mine and the old woman's—a heavy grey.

An old dresser is leaning slightly against the west wall beside a wide picture window. *There will be clothes in there*, I know, *and they will fit*. I walk to the dresser and glance out the window. Where I expected to see farmland, I instead see two pink houses that are separated in front, but strangely built into one another in back, the way one tree will sometimes grow into another. The conjoined houses are perched precariously over dull orange cliffs, with a raging ocean eating away at them from below. Stairs wind all down the cliff side. They too, are painted pink.

My giant corpse is still plainly visible, leaning drunkenly on the mountains in the distance.

The sight is disturbing, to say the least, so I turn from the window and open the dresser's top drawer to find it is filled with old He-Man toys. I pull one out and sit on the bed. It is a red action figure with eyes that bug out of his skull. His legs dangle humorously over my knee.

"You okay up there?" the old woman calls from the bottom of the stairs.

"Yes," I holler back. "Sorry, I was just playing with my toys."

"Okay," she says. "Well, the tea is just about ready, but the cookies are gonna be another few minutes. Do you want to take a shower or anything?"

"No," I say. "I'll be down in a minute. I'm just going to change my clothes real fast."

I lay back on the bed. The ceiling is a mirror, and I see myself lying in bed. My body crumbles again. I hear it cracking like the roar of distant thunder, so I race to the window just in time to see a large part of my face fall away, slamming into the ocean behind the Siamese homes beyond. A tidal wave pushes away from the fountain created where my face has dropped. The water rises, higher and higher, crashing into abandoned boats until it slams into the orange Cliffside. It spreads over and engulfs the twin houses, swallowing them whole before continuing its inland push towards the farmhouse.

"Old lady!" I shout, screaming over my shoulder as I am unable to look away from the massive rush of water heading our way. "We have to get out of here!"

"Who are you talking to?" a voice asks from behind me.

Startled, I spin around to find Vinnie the Pervert standing in the doorway. The world behind him has once again morphed into the esophageal passageway. My body once again begins straining against its casings, and I feel myself being pulled forward, thrusting full force into the meaty tunnel, back to the real world once more.

CHaPTer FIFTeen

"What the fuck was THAT?" I scream, slamming back into the trashy reality of my ex-boss's kitchen.

Moira guffaws loudly, a cigarette pinched between her fingers. Vinnie the Pervert is sitting beside me, his legs crossed. He looks rested, content. I point my finger in his smug face.

"What the hell did you just do to me?" I pat my body down. I'm thankfully still clothed, and the fact that I'm still in the kitchen gives me some small sense of security. He couldn't have done much without leaving, could he? Of course, I have no way of knowing how long he was in me. The farmhouse had seemed to take only a few minutes, maybe a half-hour, but how does that internal time measure up to real time? A day to God is one thousand years to us, my mother used to say. Did ghosting work the same way? How the hell would I know?

"Relax," Vinnie says, leaning back and yawning like a cat. "I didn't do anything bad."

"He just yanked you off," my boss offers. "No big deal."

"Oh," I say. "Well, I guess if that's all he did."

There is a brief moment where no one says anything before I leap out of my chair and shove my thumbs in Vinnie's eye sockets. He struggles, grasping my wrists and screaming, trying to pull away, but I hold firm, forcing my thumbs until the round balls of his eyes pop and spill a milky substance down the backs of my hands. Even then, I don't stop. The bone of his skull resists for a second before breaking inward, and I can feel the pulpy warmth of his brains under my fingernails. My boss is screaming, but he doesn't get up from his chair. I think he is stunned. Moira isn't doing a goddamned thing, just sitting there, watching it all unfold as if it were two ants fighting over a few crumbs of Doritos.

Vinnie finally goes limp. I hold him for a few extra seconds, kind of shaking his head in my hands. Blood and eye milk shoots out in spurts, covering my shirt and the table. Some of it even gets in the ashtray, which is funny to me for some reason. Finally, I pull my thumbs from his face, and he falls to the floor, deader than before. My boss is half to his feet, his right hand on the back of his chair behind him. Moira still doesn't move. The three of us watch as Vinnie dissolves into ectoplasm. A little ball of electric blue rises from the goop and ascends to the ceiling, passing through it with a little hiss. My boss looks at me.

"Jesus," he says. "What the hell was that about?"

"Just doing my job," I tell him, wiping my hands on the tablecloth and grabbing my still smoking cigarette from the ashtray. My boss shakes his head in disbelief, slowly lowering himself back into his seat.

"All he did was jerk you off," he mutters, half to himself.

"I don't care about that," I say, taking a long drag and watching the smoke curl up and around the little vortex spot where Vinnie's soul had finally left this earthly realm. The farmhouse swims in my peripheral vision, the fading imprint of a dream on my eyes.

"You guys have been thinking about this all wrong," I say. "You're thinking too small."

"I mean," my boss says, still staring at the spot on the ceiling. "You didn't have to fucking kill the guy."

I look at Moira, but she is judging me, too.

"You didn't even finish," She says. "It was pretty anti-climactic."

She leans forward and says, "If it had been me in there, you'd be picking cum off your pants for days."

I don't know how to take that at all.

CHAPTER SIXTEEN

A few days later, I return to Mr. Fontana's restaurant and tell him Vinnie is dead. He asks me for proof.

"It doesn't work like that," I tell him. "You just have to take my word for it. Even if I had proof, you wouldn't be able to see it."

"Well, that sucks," Sharkskin says, and we all nod in agreement.

"Sorry," I say, holding my hands out. "There's nothing I can do about it. I mean, I could show up and be like, 'I killed him, here's his head,' but you'd have no way of knowing if I was being serious or not. You couldn't see it, or even feel it. Like I said, you'll just have to take my word for it."

He mutters a quiet Japanese curse under his breath before reaching into his jacket pocket and producing a money-fat envelope. Lot of those going around lately. He holds it in the air between us, looking me in the eye for a long time before saying, "You understand I'm reluctant to pay full price without any proof, do you not?"

"I guess," I say, snatching the envelope out of his hand and climbing to my feet, "but that's pretty much how it goes."

I'm halfway to the door when Fontana says, "If this doesn't work, you'll be hearing from me again."

I turn around to face him. He is still sitting down, but there is intensity in his body that wasn't there before, like a panther about to leap. He smiles and says, "And I don't give two shits how Mafia that sounds."

CHAPTER seventeen

The park is bustling, people throwing Frisbees and jogging with headphones on, all that kind of crap. There is a dog wearing sunglasses and a baseball cap that says, "*Who farted?!*" sitting next to a hotdog cart. Two douchebags laugh on a gingham blanket. The scene feels lifted straight out of a romantic comedy from the eighties.

The crowd thins out some, near the baseball diamond. I puff on my cigarette and head for the benches. A large woman in red shorts rides her bike in front of me, and for just a second, I realize how much I don't really care about anything that ever happened in the history of the world. The entire thing could blow up, and it would hardly make any difference. Or maybe I'm just depressed? Anyway...

Parks in the city are strange places. They give this little taste of the country, but the city is right there, rising beyond the carefully planted ring of trees surrounding the ersatz slab of tranquility, standing like squat, drab monoliths in a haze just beyond the idyllic serenity of the manicured grasses and professionally installed pathways and ponds.

Thankfully, only one person is sitting on the benches, and it just happens to be the exact person I was hoping to see. I tell ya, sometimes, life just works out for the best. It almost works out *too* well. Like, if my life were a book, it would be hard to believe most of it.

The old man is lying face up on the bench, hoping for some young woman to come along and sit on his face. I sit down beside him and crush my cigarette with my foot.

"Do you remember me?" I ask.

"Sure do," he says pleasantly, "you're the young man that keeps interrupting my sexual proclivities."

"That's right," I say, "and I'm sorry about that, but I think I may have an idea of how to make that up to you and make myself a shitload of money in the process."

I wish I were still smoking my cigarette. I put it out too early, and now I feel like this would all seem much cooler if I was still smoking, but I'm not, and I don't want to light another one right now, so there's nothing I can do about it but keep going without one.

"What's your name?" I ask.

The old man sits up and holds out his hand.

"Jerry," he says.

"Well, Jerry," I say, taking his hand and kind of pulling him in a bit closer. "How would you like to feel something again?"

A throat a car crash angelic singing meld with the feel of grey hair on my temples and a rainbow on the outskirts of my vision pulls me down into the warm embrace of home once more.

"Excuse me a moment," I say before leaving the prostitute sitting on the hotel bed to go and see what the hell Jerry is hollering about in the bathroom. "What is going on in here?"

"Is she pretty?" Jerry asks, sitting naked on the toilet, rubbing his hands together excitedly. "What color is her hair?"

"Why are you naked?" I ask. "That doesn't make any sense! You're going to be using *my* body, remember? There is absolutely no reason for you to be naked right now."

"I was always partial to redheads, myself," Jerry says, totally ignoring me. "They have a touch of craziness to them."

"Look," I say, putting my hands firmly on his shoulders and looking him right in the eyes. "You have got to get it together. You know how this works. I'm going to tell her all about your weird-ass face-sitting fetish and figure out how much it costs. I'll pay her and then excuse myself. You enter me, go out there and let her sit on my face until you're done, or whatever, and you come back in here and leave my body, understand?"

Jerry nods, biting his bottom lip.

"Okay," he says. "Yeah, yeah, okay. Sorry, you're right." He laughs and says, "I'm just so fucking nervous, you know?"

"Me too," I say.

I'm already in the house, this time, still looking out the window. The flood is gone, and the pink houses are still there, but other than that, it seems as if no time has passed. The drawer to the dresser is hanging open, but the He-Man action figures are gone this time. I see several flannel work shirts in their place, the sleeves threadbare but still holding. Another drawer reveals several Jules Verne books, all of them First Editions. I flip open a copy of *20,000 Leagues Under the Sea* and read the word "staircase" before hearing several voices floating up from downstairs.

Setting the book carefully back in the drawer, I slip on one of the work shirts and head down the stairs to investigate.

The kitchen smells of mint and roast meat. A pot boils over on the stove as the old woman washes two enormous carrots in the sink. Sitting at the table, spooning soup into his mouth from a large bowl, is a tall black man of slender build, wearing a thin work shirt similar to mine. Even though I have never seen him before, I know him instinctively. His name is Anthony Burt. He is one year older than me, and manages to put everyone around him in a good mood whenever he smiles. I sit down beside him and pat him on the back.

"How's it going, Anthony?" I ask as he turns and smiles up at me. "Long time no see."

"Thomas?" He says, hugging me with one arm and stirring his spoon through his soup with the other. "My god, I feel like it's been *ages!*"

The old woman sets a bowl of soup down in front of me and dries her hands on her apron.

Smiling down at us, she says in a faraway voice, "It's so good to have my boys back home again."

I am just about to say something when there is a muffled thump from upstairs. It sounds like someone dropped a bowling ball. Then several tennis balls drop.

"Oh, Jesus Christ," the old woman says, running over and grabbing a broom. She comes back over to where we are sitting and starts banging the broom against the ceiling, shouting, "You keep it down up there, or I'll come and drag you outta this boy *myself!*"

The thumping stops. Anthony and I laugh. We finish our soup, and the old woman tells us to "run along and let me do my dishes."

The two of us retire to the front porch and sit on a nailsick porch swing. Anthony produces two hand-rolled cigarettes from his breast pocket, and we sit and smoke and watch as tiny bits of my corpse break off and fall to the ocean in the distance. Anthony, too, has a giant corpse propped up against the mountain. His lips have peeled back in a desiccated snarl.

"What's that over there?" I ask him, pointing towards an old barn across the dirt path.

"That's where the Barnfather lives," Anthony says. "We're not supposed to go in there, but I did once, a few years ago. Wish I hadn't. That place scared the shit outta me."

"Truth be told," he says, taking a drag of his cigarette, "I don't know how you could've dreamed something up like that. You didn't have a mind like that when we were kids."

Just like that, it all comes back to me: Anthony Burt. I hadn't seen him since he and his family moved to Germany back when we were eight years old. We had been inseparable, growing up in California, Fort Ord, California, to be exact. A military base near the Salinas Valley. The same Salinas Valley Steinbeck wrote about in *East of Eden*. I guess Anthony has grown up in my subconscious, becoming the fine man I now see before me.

I look at the barn again. The red paint is chipped, and in some places, old pallets have been nailed to cover gaping holes in the walls. We hear a deep rumble that I at first think is our bodies collapsing, but soon realize it is coming from the barn. It is a heavy, deep sound, like ten million cows mooing in unison. A primal, angry sound that rattles our eardrums and clacks our teeth together.

"The Barnfather," I say before the sky pulls tight and snaps, revealing a gaping vagina that slowly lowers over my face like a death mask.

CHAPTER EIGHTEEN

TV Newscaster: *"We go now live to the scene."*

Reporter: *"Thank you, Dale. I'm here live at Shorty's Arcade where yet another Ghost User has committed an unprovoked sexual attack."*

The camera pans quickly to the left. A haggard teen with bad skin and two-day stubble stands with his hands shoved in the front pocket of an oversized hoodie.

Teen: *"Yeah, I mean, I was just standing there, talkin' to my boy Tony, when all-a sudden this crazy dude comes runnin' over, and he starts rubbin' himself against the bartender. At first, I was just like, 'what?' but then I was like, 'whoa, homeboy got his dick out, y'know what I mean?"*

Reporter: *"Do you suspect the man was on Ghost? Do you suppose that had anything to do with the attack?"*

Teen: *"Prolly was, I dunno. I mean, I don't know too much about it, but I know it's bad stuff."*

Jerry huffs angrily beside me. He keeps losing focus and falling through the lawn chair set up in the living room.

"Ten to one, that kid knows more about Ghost than a room full of reporters," he says, pulling himself up and gesticulating angrily at the TV.

Jerry and I are now drug kingpins. Taking the idea of Tenements, or whatever stupid name it had before, I created a faux drug empire selling talcum powder to halfwits and a few hours good time to a bunch of dead guys. With Jerry as my partner, we have cornered a market where we own everything, even the corner. We are rich beyond our wildest dreams, and I am riddled with sexually transmitted diseases. We sit, watching TV in our dingy apartment, slurping ramen out of yellow bowls, waiting for the night shift to start.

Ghost.

Yeah. That's us. A fine, white powder, smooth as talc. Because it *is* talc. The "drug" isn't the powder. It's the ghosts. Jerry finds a ghost willing and responsible enough to possess someone. Then, we find someone looking to get high and sell them a bag of talcum powder. The dead person is right there behind me the whole time, of course, and they just follow the person home and jump in them whenever they sniff the talc. Bingo bango, it takes tutu mango.

The cops hate us, of course. Or, they hate me, I guess. Jerry is dead, so they probably don't feel one way or the other about him.

So it goes.

On the TV, the Chief of Police, Colin McMaster, fills the screen with a face full of pockmarks and a neck filled with fat as he mumbles into a phallic gathering of microphones on a pedestal.

"We do know that the attacker was under the influence of the underground drug Necrothoramine, commonly known as 'Ghost.'" He says. *"He did not appear to know the woman, and we still have no reason to believe the attack was premeditated. That's all for now, thank you."*

65

Back in the studio, the Anchorwoman is shaking her head in disgust. Her mucus-orange blazer bedazzled with rhinestones. She straightens a stack of papers on the desk before saying, *"This is far from the first attack committed by an assailant under the influence of Ghost, the newest street drug to terrorize our fair city. Police still have no leads as to who is smuggling the substance in, nor do they have any clue where it is being manufactured..."*

I turn the television off and lean into the sofa cushions.

"Idiots," I say, more to myself than to anyone, but Jerry perks up at my words.

"That's what I was trying to say!" he yells. "Every time one of these guys goes into a sex frenzy, they manage to pull out the most drug-addled mother fucker they can find on the scene to stammer his way through an eye-witness account. Do you know why they do that?" he asks, wheeling on me. "Because it's all *propaganda*! They're trying to force the viewer to subconsciously connect Ghost with meth heads and junkies. Who else but an obvious drug addict can *possibly* know what's going on, eh? And the god damned public eats it up! Look at that fat neck police chief they pulled away from the trough! *'Necrothoramine'*?! Where did they come up with that? It's fucking *talcum powder*! They just make up shit like that so the public won't panic when they say they have *no idea* how we're doing this. So I ask you, who are real idiots?"

"Everybody, Jerry," I sigh. "Everybody."

Jerry laughs.

"Who've we got on shift tonight?" I ask him.

"We've got Eddie the Panty-Sniffer on the lower East Side; he shouldn't be too much trouble."

"I guess I'm going to the lower East Side then," I climb to my feet and stretch. My back pops. "We on for tonight?"

"Of course," Jerry says, suddenly all smiles. "I've got twins coming over tonight. Did you hear me? Twins!"

Jerry and I have a special partnership set up. I provide him with a host body and a place to live, and he hooks me up with trips to the farmhouse. Every time he takes me over, I get a little deeper into that other place. Last night, Anthony and I found an old fishing well behind the abandoned chicken coop. We made a rod and reel out of sticks and rope and spent the day pulling all manner of things from the water. At one point, Anthony fought to reel in a milk crate filled with G.I. Joe action figures. We played War with them and made a base for them out of mud. They flopped around out of the water, and we felt bad, so we threw them back when we were done.

I grab my backpack and fill it with plastic bags of baby powder. Jerry is already glued to the TV again.

On the way out the door, I say, "Do me a favor and wear a condom this time, please? Nobody is going to want to sleep with us if you keep giving me crabs."

Jerry waves me away dismissively.

"No promises," he says.

CHAPTER NINETEEN

The cops can't track where Ghost is manufactured because it isn't being manufactured anywhere. Half the time, it isn't even talcum powder. Any white substance will do. It doesn't matter. People just want something to shove up their noses. They want an escape, and nothing provides a better escape than Ghost. While the details are different for everyone, the main points are the same: you find yourself falling down a deep hallway, until you end up in another place. It is universally peaceful, despite everyone reporting they saw their body decaying in the distance.

In the beginning, it took some time to work the kinks out. For starters, we had no set limit on how long a spirit could remain inside someone. That's where Ghost started developing its first bad reputation. A dead person would be on a roll in somebody's body for three or four days, and the person would lose their job, or miss their kid's recital or something.

Jerry had to follow the dead people around for a while, making sure they left in a reasonable amount of time, but not such a short amount of time the customer would feel ripped off. There were rumors on the street of people "cutting" Ghost with impurities, which was ridiculous, because there wasn't anything "impure" to add. They started saying the new Ghost was "weak sauce." So we extended the amount of time again.

Finally, we settled on a six-hour trip, uniform for everyone, across the board.

That lasted about ten minutes.

Dead people, in general, aren't terribly concerned with death. As far as they see it, the worst is over, so who cares if some medium or whatever is pissed off? What are they gonna do about it, kill them?

Well, yeah, actually.

Turns out, Jerry's pretty well connected in the spirit underworld, and he is a diligent record keeper to boot. He knew the names and local hangouts of every murdered malcontent and elderly lothario we ever hired, and when they messed up or ruined someone's life, I was on it.

In the first year alone, I personally exorcised two hundred horny former humans, and earned myself the nickname, The Other Reaper.

Of course, killing the ghosts that caused the problems didn't help the people whose lives we'd destroyed, but it ensured it wouldn't happen to anyone else. And anyway, drugs are bad, and those people shouldn't have bought them from me in the first place if they had to go to work or a birthday party. That's just bad planning on their part.

By year two, aside from a few mistakes here and there, things were running fairly smoothly. We were the only Ghost dealers in the world, and realistically, what we were actually selling was relatively harmless compared to other drugs on the market.

So, I mean, whatever.

CHaPTer TweNTy

The lower East Side smells the way you'd imagine the Employee Port-A-Potty might smell at a carnival. Rats battle it out with seagulls for whatever scraps of garbage the junkies drop as they pass out near the Scrapyard dumpsters. Tourists only appear when they are so lost they are just hoping to make it back to the hotel in one piece. When the bus drives through, the driver doesn't stop, she just slows down and opens the door, and I jump out, tucking and rolling. So, naturally, it is the obvious choice for a drug deal.

Eddie the Panty-Sniffer is slumped against a rotted pier railing, wearing a long trench coat as I approach. His comically nonchalant posture is belied by his nervous, searching eyes. At six-foot-two inches, one hundred fifteen pounds, he looks like a man trying very hard to look like he *doesn't* have a gun.

When he catches my eye, he leaps to attention, walking in quick, nervous steps and grabbing my hand hard, and jacking it up and down wildly in a frantic greeting.

"Hiya, man, hiya," he says. "You been here long? I mean, no, of course not. You just got here. HAHAHA-HAHA! So, yeah. Anyway, are you ready to do this? Like, do you have a buyer set up? Where's the guy, man?"

"Jesus, Eddie, calm down," I shout. A Longshoreman getting a blowjob in a nearby alley shouts for me to keep it down, and I apologize.

Pulling my hand from Eddie's grip, I say, "There's a buyer, okay? There's always a buyer. Just, you know, be cool, man."

"I'm cool," Eddie pats his jacket and tries to look re-laxed, like he is only acting frazzled because he's trying to find his lighter or something. "Hey, I'm cool."

Somewhere, a foghorn blows. As if on cue, fog rolls in. Eddie shivers.

"He's coming," he says.

Addicts have a sort of extra sense when a fix is close by. Their bodies tense up, then relax, a sort of mus-cle breathing that conveys calmness and anticipation in equal measure. Eddie is suddenly quiet, and from out of the fog, a figure emerges.

A first, it's just a sort of dark blue silhouette, but soon it becomes a heavyset man in a thick, blue sweater and black stocking cap. The man walks confidently at first, but his step falters momentarily when he eyes us. Or me, I guess. Whatever. A sausage-fat finger points at me.

"You Thomas?" he asks.

"Yeah," I say, and Eddie punches me on the arm.

"Never give your real name, boss!" he whispers. "Al-ways use an alias."

"What difference does it make?" I mutter. Then, to the figure, I say, "You Glenn?"

"Yeah."

We approach one another and shake hands. Glenn's palms are calloused and dry, and I have to bite my tongue to keep from mentioning the thing about the fish with the chapped lips. Eddie shuffles nervously from one foot to the other behind me. Glenn clears his throat.

"You picked a hell of a meeting place," he says.

"I like the general ambiance," I tell him. "Did you bring the money?"

"Yeah," he says. "Did you bring the Ghost?"

"Don't answer that," Eddie says. "It's not too late! Come up with a different name, quick! While he's distracted!"

"He's not distracted," I say.

Glenn looks at me.

"What?" he asks.

"Nothing," I said. "Just thinking of a song I wrote. You wanted four bags, right?'

"That's right," Glenn says, his words coming slow and deliberate. "I want you to sell me four bags of Ghost for four hundred dollars, cash. Can you do that?'

"I don't like this, boss," Eddie says. He reaches into his coat pocket and pulls out a pair of heavily soiled underwear. He shoves them under his nose and takes a long, deep whiff.

"Shut up," I say. "I tell you, it's fine!"

"Come again?" Glenn asks. "Can you sell me the Ghost or what?"

"Yes, damn it, I can."

I drop the backpack and open the zipper. One of the bags has come open from when I jumped off the bus, and the powder goes everywhere. Glenn leaps back from the powder like it's a snake. He holds his wrist up to his face and says, "We got it."

Suddenly, the Longshoreman and the Prostitute come racing out of the alley, guns pointed at my chest, and they're all screaming, "*Get down on the ground! Get down on the ground!*"

I put my hands up and ask Eddie what I should do.

"What are you, simple?" he says, panties on his head. "Get down on the fucking ground!"

I get down on the fucking ground. Glenn leans down and puts his knee in my back, cuffing my hands. I look at the Longshoreman and see that, even though he is holding a gun and has a badge hanging from his belt buckle, his fly is down, and his dick is hanging out. Even though he is a part of this sting operation to take me down, I have to admire his commitment to the role.

I mean, he could've just acted like he was getting a blowjob, but no. He and his partner went that extra mile, and I can't help but respect them both.

They really went above and beyond.

CHAPTER TWENTY-ONE

The city jail is not at all like *Night Court*, and the cops are not terribly friendly.

I don't mean to suggest that they are rude or anything. In fact, in between clubbing me with the phone book while I'm strapped to a chair and tasing me, they've been the model of hospitality. That said, were I to leave a *Yelp!* review, it would be one or two stars, at most.

On the way here, I asked Eddie to get Jerry and bring him down to the Police Station. He had ridden part of the way in the squad car with me, offering advice on how to deal with the cops, which consisted mostly of me not saying anything to anyone for any reason, no matter what. He kept saying that: no matter what.

I didn't know what he meant by it until I ignored the first officer who asked me where I manufactured Ghost. I kept my mouth shut, taking the advice of a man who—so far as I was aware—had the last of "Panty-Sniffer."

In hindsight, this was a bad move.

Now, strapped to a metal folding chair in an interrogation room with a bloody nose and two heavily cauliflowered ears, I consider just lying, telling them whatever they want to hear so I can go back to my cell and piss blood for a while. Something about Glenn's face, though—now that he is out of his "druggy" costume and back in his police fatigues—makes me defiant. So, when he asks me, again, where I'm making the stuff, I say, "at your mom's house."

He drives his fist into my gut, and I vomit. It gets all over me, and it gets all over him, and he steps back with his arms out in front of him, looking at my puke in disgust.

"You got it all over me, you fucking moron!" he screams.

"Well, excuse me, Mr. Perfect," I say. "I guess you've never made a mistake."

Glenn tries wiping my puke off his arms with his hands, but it just spreads around more.

Finally, he says, "Get this scum out of my sight."

They take me to my cell, and I collapse on the cot. I am almost completely in a comfortable fetal position when I hear something outside.

"Thomas, you in there?" someone says.

The window in my cell is small, with four bars in it, and high up on the wall. Slowly, painfully, I climb to my feet, cradling my busted ribcage, and peek over the sill to see jerry standing there. Eddie the Panty-Sniffer is standing beside him.

"I found him, Thomas," he says. "Just like you said."

"Nice work, Eddie," I say. "What are you guys doing out there?"

"We're just trying to find a way in," Jerry says.

"You're dead," I say.

"Oh yeah," they say in unison before just walking through the wall and standing there looking at me.

75

"Sorry about that," Jerry says. "What with everything else going on, I guess I forgot I'd been dead for forty years."

He clears his throat sheepishly.

"Or however long it's been," he says.

"It's been twelve years for me," Eddie volunteers. I nod.

"It'll be a few minutes yet," I say, "before I join you guys."

Jerry helps me down onto the cot and says, "Don't you be talking that way, boss. We're gonna get you out of here. See, Eddie and me? We got a plan!"

CHAPTER TWENTY-TWO

Eddie leaves the cell, leaving Jerry behind to tell me the
plan.

However before Jerry can tell me anything, a guard
shows up and unlocks my cell.

"Act cool," he says.

I try to stand up, but my left knee gives out, and
I crumble to the floor. Jerry tries to help me up, but
touching something and making it move requires a lot
of concentration for the dead, and Jerry can't muster the
energy. He's too distracted by everything else going on.

"On your feet, motherfucker," the guard says, nervously shaking the keys in his hand. "This guy is fighting me."

"No," I say. "I'm not resisting. I just can't move."

"Not you," the guard says. "The guy I'm in. This guy.
He's fighting me."

"What?" I ask.

"It's Eddie," Jerry says. "That's part of the plan."

"Oh."

"I'm going to have to take you over," Jerry tells me. "It's
the only way. You'll have to take all the pain with you,

though, when you go. Otherwise, I won't be able to move either."

"Okay," is all I say, and Jerry leaps into my mouth.

CHAPTER TWENTY-TWO

CHAPTER TWENTY-THREE

The farmhouse bed is warm and safe, and my body is broken within it. Somehow, Jerry shifted me into my subconscious with all my pain intact. The old woman helped me to my room and layered the bed with heavy comforters and too many pillows. She placed a blue velvet teddy bear beside my head and asked me if I remembered him.

"Of course," I said, half-unconscious from the pain. "It's Mr. Bear."

I pull Mr. Bear closer to myself and look out the window, my vision swimming. Outside, my mountainous carcass is in shambles. The flesh has become dry and desiccated, the lips peeling away from the teeth, exposing a hideous gum line being picked apart by seabirds. Miles long strands of hair fall, hitting the earth below with an earthquake hum.

A knock on the door, and Anthony enters. He is holding a G.I. Joe, still wet, the legs kicking. He approaches the bed and sits gingerly on the edge.

"I caught this for you," he says, holding out the G.I. Joe. "The old woman said you were hurt. I thought it might help you feel better."

My mouth is dry, but I say, "Thanks."

"Who did this to you?"

"A cop."

The Barnfather rumbles in the barn. The entire house shakes. Anthony climbs to his feet and looks out the window.

"He's worried about you," he says. "He's been more active today. Even before you got here, I think he knew you were in trouble."

Turning from the window, he sets the toy on the dresser and heads for the door.

Before he leaves, he turns and says," "I'll bring a bowl up for the G.I. Joe. Try to get some rest."

"Okay," I say, and he turns to leave.

"Hey, Anthony?" I ask.

"Yeah, buddy?"

"Thanks."

He smiles.

"Don't mention it."

A few hours later, the old woman comes up with a bowl of chicken noodle soup. I must have dozed off. The light outside is dim, rimmed in pinks and purples. I see the G.I. Joe swimming in a bowl of murky water beside the bed next to the old woman's head. She sits down beside me and ladles warm soup into my mouth. After a few bites, watching me choke and chew and cough and wheeze, she puts her hand on my forehead and clucks her tongue.

"You're not getting any better," she says.

"Is that unusual?" I ask.

"It isn't good," she says.

She calls for Anthony, and then there he is. Time is slipping away from me. He seems to materialize beside the bed the moment he's called. The old woman takes him to the corner of the room, and they confer with one another in hushed tones, nervous looks in my direction pepper their talk.

Finally, the old woman says, "Then it's decided. You get him on his feet. I'm gonna go put on my shawl. I'll meet you downstairs in five minutes."

The Barnfather rumbles throughout the house. Anthony walks up to me with his hands in his pockets.

"Hey, buddy," he says. "So, the old woman is getting a little worried about you. She says we need to take you outside."

"Am I dying?"

Anthony shrugs.

"Honestly, I don't know. She seems to think you're not healing fast enough, and she's worried you might be in for a longer visit."

"Is that a problem?" I ask. "I've always been able to stay as long as I wanted before."

Then, I say, "I think I kind of thought I lived here."

"You do," Anthony says. "Or, I mean, you will. Some day. It's not the kind of thing you want to do right now. Moving home again."

"Is that what this is?" I ask. "Home?"

"Kind of," Anthony says. "See, you did live here before. A long time ago, before you were born, and you'll come home again someday. But like I said, it's not something you want to do right now."

The G.I. Joe flops in the bowl, splashing water on the dresser. Anthony looks at me and smiles.

"Do you understand what I'm saying?'

"I think so," I say, even though I am not so sure I do.

The old woman calls from downstairs. Anthony puts his hands on my shoulders and helps me sit up. The pain in my ribcage is explosive, and I am torn through with another coughing fit. Blood sprays from my mouth,

spattering the fish bowl, the comforters, and Anthony's
face. He doesn't bother wiping it off.

"Oh man," he says. "Come on, try to stand up. We don't
have much time."

Climbing slowly to my feet, I ask, "where are you
taking me?"

"We're going," he says, "to see the Barnfather."

82

CHaPTeR TWenTY-FouR

After struggling down the stairs and out the front door, Anthony and the old woman push and prod me towards the barn. My body is crumbling behind me, raining rotten flesh all over the distant mountains like cadaverous dandruff. A loud bang fills the air, and the old woman cries out, frightened.

"Hurry," she shouts. "Whatever they're doing, it's getting worse."

The barn looms up in front of us. The boards rattle and shake with the deep, throaty grumblings of the Barnfather. Crop-dusters rocket down from the clouds, dowsing the cornfield again and again in toxic, red mist.

Another explosion and a quarter-size hole appears on my stomach.

"Oh shit," is the last thing Anthony says before I'm pulled back through the tunnel and find myself prone over a dining room table in a Tiki bar, with Jerry standing over me.

"What the fuck just happened?" I shout.

"We've got to run, boss," Jerry says. "Eddie lost control of the guard. He shot you!"

I want to ask what the hell he's talking about, but it clears itself up before I do.

Eddie is standing against a far corner, dirty panties wrapped around his face, and the guard he had possessed is standing in the center of the room, gun drawn and pointed right at me.

"I told you not to move!" he screams.

I sit up on the table, bumping my head on a rubber shrunken head hanging from the overhead light.

"I wasn't planning on it," I say. Then, looking at Jerry, I say, "*This* was your plan?"

Jerry shrugs.

"I was planning on fucking twins," he says somewhat indignantly.

"I said shut up!" the guard screams, stepping closer and managing to point the gun even more at my face.

"Sorry," I said. "Not to nitpick, but you said not to move. You never said shut up."

"He did, actually," Eddie says, his voice muffled by a pair of pink panties emblazoned with the words, *cheeky bitch*. "When Jerry was trying to fight him in your body."

"I said shut the fuck up," the guard screams again.

"Sorry," I say.

So, I've been shot. The plan has fallen apart, and I'm in a Tiki bar somewhere.

Okay.

That's fine.

So it goes.

"So," I say, looking at the guard and trying not to look like anything other than a totally cooperative hostage on the verge of what is very likely his last moments on earth. "What do we do now?"

"Just stay right there," the guard says. "Keep your mouth shut and tell me what the hell is happening.

Where are we? What happened to the old lady at the beach?"

I nod. I see. When I am possessed, I go to the farmhouse. For him, it's a beach. Eddie lost control, and the poor guy found himself in this tacky Tiki place, with an escaped drug peddler standing in front of him. That'd be a tough pill for anyone to swallow.

"I can't help you, boss," Jerry says. "That last one took a lot out of me, and I think your body would reject me, banged up as bad as it is."

"Eddie?" I ask, but he's gone. I don't know when he left, but there's nothing where he was but a pile of dirty underwear.

"Who is Eddie?" the guard shouts.

"I'm Eddie," a voice says behind me.

I turn to look, and there is Sharkskin, standing in a three-piece suit and holding a shotgun.

"Sharkskin!" I shout. "Your name is Eddie?! That's so weird!"

"Why is that weird?" Sharkskin asks. "Eddie Flavio Fazio. What's wrong with that?"

"Nothing," I say. "It's a good name."

"Shut the fuck up, both of you!" the guard screams, alternately pointing the gun at me and Eddie Flavio Fazio. "I don't want to hear another word until someone tells me what the fuck is going on here!"

Another door opens, and who, to my wondering eyes, should appear but Mr. Antonio Fontana himself! He's holding a Tiki mug shaped like a Moai and is wearing a tacky white jacket over a red Hawaiian shirt with yellow flowers.

"I would like to know the answer to that myself," he says.

And then, Eddie Flavio Fazio pulls the trigger and reduces the confused guard to a bloody arterial spray and a pair of legs in blue pants that stand comically upright for a beat before crumbling to the crowd and pouring their contents all over the white tile floor.

"Clean up in aisle five," Jerry says.

CHAPTER TWENTY-FIVE

"Ah, Mr. Johansson," Antonio says while Eddie Flavio Fazio mops up what used to be the top half of the guard. "Long time no see. Tell me, how did you come to find yourself in my restaurant again?"

"This is your restaurant?" I ask. "I thought it was an Italian place?"

"It was," he says, looking around proudly. "You see, after you left, I got to thinking. And you know what?"

"No," I say. "What?"

"You were right. It was a little weird for me to be running an Italian place. So, I decided to make a few changes. I went with a Tiki theme. What do you think of it?"

"It's great," I say. "Big fan. Huge."

Then, I say," Forgive me for changing the subject, but I appear to be bleeding to death on one of your tables."

Antonio looks down at my bloody mess of a body and nods.

"You certainly do appear to be doing just that," he says.

He takes a long, slow sip of his Moai head, looking me steadily in the eyes the whole time. Then, he carefully sets the mug down beside me, smacks his lips, and goes, "Ahh! Delicious!"

"I don't like where this is going, boss," Jerry says next to me.

"I don't either, Jerry," I say.

"You shouldn't," Antonio says. I look at him.

"I can't see whoever you're talking to, Mr. Johansson," he tells me. "But I'm assuming it is a ghost of some kind, and I'm assuming they just told you they don't like the look of this."

"You assume correctly," I say, laying back down on the table and applying pressure to the bullet hole in my stomach. "Are you going to kill me?"

"Doesn't seem like I need to," he answers. "That guard seems to have done that already."

"So I assume you're not going to help me?"

"You assume correctly," he says, proud of bringing it back around like that.

I nod.

"May I ask why?" I ask.

"I think you know."

"Well," Jerry says, "assuming we don't?"

"Assuming we don't?" I ask.

"Tell your friend to leave us," Antonio says.

"Jerry, you may go."

"But, boss, I don't think..."

"It's okay, Jerry," I tell him. "You've done all you could. You've been a good friend, and a great partner. I've never really been happy in life, I don't think, until I met you. You showed me the farmhouse. You helped me sell drugs. You gave me herpes. You've been a good friend."

Eddie Flavio Fazio looks up from his mopping and says, "You've got herpes?"

Antonio holds his hand up and shakes his head, "Eddie, please. Give him a moment to say goodbye to his friend."

Jerry puts his hand on my chest. He's got tears in his eyes.

I've never seen a ghost cry. Even the ones I'd ripped apart. The ones I'd run through a paper shredder. The ones I'd curb-stomped, bludgeoned, chainsawed, impaled, decapitated. Not one of them ever shed a tear. But Jerry? Leaning over me, his eyes loving and kind, the dirty old pervert sheds a series of milky white orbs, like tiny, translucent tapioca pearls. They roll down his cheeks and rise into the air, floating like feathers up to the ceiling. It is beautiful.

"Boss," he says. "Alive or dead, you're the best friend I ever had. Thank you for letting me rent your penis to have sex with all those people."

"It was my pleasure, Jerry," I say, and we embrace.

When we pull apart, Jerry wipes the tears from his eyes and walks towards the door, stopping to air hump Eddie Flavio Fazio from behind while he mops before moving on.

After a moment, Antonio Fontana says, "Is he gone?"

"Yeah," I say, wiping my eyes. "He's gone."

"I'm just going to say this once," he tells me. "I only heard one half of that conversation. I know that. But it sounds like the two of you had a fucked up relationship."

I laugh.

"Yeah," I say. "I guess we did."

Eddie Flavio Fazio grunts, puts the mop away, plops down in the chair beside his boss, and says, "Finished!"

"Okay then," Antonio says, clapping his hands together. "Shall we get started?"

"Started with what?" I ask.

"With killing you, Mr. Johansson," he says. "With killing you."

CHAPTER TWENTY-SIX

"Technically," I say as Eddie Flavio Fazio straps me to a metal table in the kitchen, "I did what you paid me to do."

Antonio Fontana is busy making himself another cocktail. He shakes rum and pineapple juice with ice in a metal cup, then pours the drink into a parrot-shaped Tiki mug.

"Vinnie the Snitch is dead," I say. "Again."

Antonio opens a tiny umbrella and sets it in the parrot's head. He puts a straw in it and takes a sip, screwing his face up and exhaling sharply.

"Man," he says. "That's a good drink!"

"I dug my thumbs into his eyes," I explain. "His soul looked like a blue ball."

"Is he strapped in, Eddie?" he says, pulling up a bamboo chair and scooching it until he's a few inches from my face.

"Yeah," Eddie answers. "Though I don't think it'll matter much. He's basically dead right now. He ain't going nowhere."

"Thank you, Eddie," Antonio says.

"Yeah, thanks, Eddie," I say.

Eddie smacks me, hard, across the mouth. I feel a few teeth get knocked loose. Stars. A momentary, hazy flash of the farmhouse.

"That's enough, Eddie," Antonio says. "I don't want him dying until he understands why."

"I said I understood," I tell him.

When they'd muscled me into the kitchen from the bar, I'd gathered that the problems with the restaurant hadn't been solved with the second death of Vinnie the Snitch. Apparently, the ghost, or specter, or spirit, or whatever had continued knocking stuff off the walls, spoiling dinners, and generally being a pain in the ass even after I'd collected my money.

"I told you," I say as Antonio sips his parrot. "It was probably that Japanese guy that was hanging around. He seemed upset you hadn't called 911 fast enough."

"A Japanese ghost," Antonio says. "Haunting an Italian restaurant? Please, Mr. Johansson. You're embarrassing yourself."

"It's true," is all I say.

Truth be told. I don't really care anymore. Death. Life. Same difference. I just want all this to be over. Life. This. All of it. But one thing is still bothering me.

"Who was Moira?" I ask. "I thought she was going to play a bigger part in all of this."

"For now," Antonio says, climbing to his feet. "Let's forget about Moira, whoever she may be. Let's focus," he puts on a pair of black rubber gloves and pulls a meat cleaver from a chopping block. "On you and I."

He had said he wanted to explain why he was going to kill me. Instead, he just turns around and brings the meat cleaver down on my face.

CHAPTER TWENTY-SEVEN

Death brings an immediate release.

It's like I'd been holding a fart for the last thirty-eight years, and I'd finally just let it rip.

Antonio Fontana is standing over my corpse. My head has fallen to the floor and rolled over by a box of umbrellas. The box says, **TIKI UMBRELLAS. 200 UNITS**.

Looking up at where I'm assuming he thinks my ghost must be, he says, "that's what we do to people who fuck with the Mafia, Mr. Johansson."

"I knew you were Mafia!" I shout, pointing my finger angrily at him.

"I can't hear you," he says. "But I'm assuming you just said, 'oh my goodness! You were in the Mafia? I had no idea!' Well, surprise, Mr. Johansson!"

I snort, shaking my head.

"That's not what I said at all," I say. "Idiot."

Jerry appears, walking through the kitchen wall, and smiles sheepishly at me.

"Hey, boss," he says. "I couldn't leave you. Death can be confusing. I figured you could use some help."

I run over and give him a big hug.

"I'm glad you stayed, Jerry," I say.

I'm about to ask him what we should do next when a wide, sore-throat colored tunnel appears behind Jerry. Antonio is still delivering his villainous monologue, but we're not paying any attention. I stick my hand in the tunnel.

"What is it?" I ask Jerry.

"That's the light people talk about," he says.

"Do we have to go through?"

"I didn't," he says. "I don't think I was ready."

"What's on the other side?"

Jerry shrugs.

"Beats me," he says.

Then, nudging my ribs, he asks with a smile, "Wanna find out?"

I smile.

"Together?" I ask.

"Together," he says.

Here's a joke for you: "Why did the two dead drug dealers cross the threshold between worlds?"

Answer: "To get to the other side."

EPILOGUE

Life on the farmhouse is slow, idyllic. A paradise.

Jerry and the old woman are a couple now, and they have wild, noisy old people sex every night. Anthony and I have sleepovers, and we hide under the covers and laugh at their grunts and thumps. Afternoons, we go fishing for toys in the pond out back.

When we first arrived, Jerry and I were taken to the barn to meet the Barnfather for the first time. Anthony had tried to prepare me, but words do not adequately convey the sheer horror one experiences when meeting a giant, multi-tentacled cow god meditating in a barn in the afterlife.

Surrounded by Tiki torches and chicken wire, the Barnfather sat cross-legged, a flaming halo surrounding the ten-thousand horns encircling his head. Several dozen tentacles protruded from his back, each tipped with the heads of people I had known in life. My old boss sneered from the end of an octopus arm. Moira dangled from another. There was my mother. My father. Vinnie the Snitch. Eddie the Pervert. Eddie Flavio Fazio and

Antonio Fontana smiled down from a long tentacle that forked at the end to accommodate them both.

There were even a few faces I didn't recognize. People that had mattered to Jerry.

His wife. The redheaded prostitute from years ago. And, bizarrely, Eddie the Panty-Sniffer again. The only person important enough to appear twice.

"Come, my children," the Barnfather said. "Come and suckle at the teats that made the world. Come and be infants again, in paradise."

He moved the two appendages that had appeared the most cow-like, and exposed a massive, fleshy milk bag dripping with liquid manna. Jerry and I didn't hesitate. We'd raced to the warm embrace of the Barnfather. We wrapped our lips around his udders and pulled deeply, grateful for the milk that flowed so freely from him to us.

Afterward, we'd been welcomed home in grand style. The fields had been dusted and harvested, and we ate corn fertilized with every second of our lives. We drank milk from the ever-flowing teats of God.

And, for dessert, the old woman made us cupcakes.

Death moves along, slow and steady. We are happy in this moment. Happy and alive.

Or dead.

Whatever.

Acknowledgments

While I don't really remember where the idea for this book came from, I know I couldn't have written it without the help and input of the following people: First and foremost, Matt and everyone at Planet Bizarro for all your hard work and dedication; Second, I would like to thank my bonsai buddy, Fontanimal, without whom I would've kept the dirty bits secret a bit longer; And finally, Shailah, who pushes me to write better so I'll stop complaining about everything. Thank you all.

ABOUT THE AUTHOR

Dustin Reade lives and breathes in Port Angeles, Washington. He writes weird stories and books, and some of them are *Bad Hotel*, *Grambo*, and *The Canal*. His short stories have appeared in over one hundred anthologies and ezines, and have recently been translated into Polish. He has a degree in Funerary Services Education, and he mostly eats junk food. When not writing weird stories, he creates experimental music in all genres under the moniker, "Call Me Dusty." He can feel it when you Google him, so please don't do it after 2 a.m Mountain Time.

OTHER TITLES FROM PLANET BIZARRO

Peculiar Monstrosities – A Bizarre Horror Anthology

A stripper's boyfriend bites off more than he can chew during a hiking trip.
A man looking for love marries a jukebox.
A popular children's character is brought to life, but something isn't quite right.
A shady exchange on a Kaiju cruise leads to catastrophic complications.

Peculiar Monstrosities is packed with fourteen exquisitely crafted stories from new and established authors of Bizarro fiction.

Featuring tales by: Kevin J. Kennedy, Zoltan Komor, Shelly Lyons, Tim Anderson, Tim O'Neal, Gregory L.

Norris, Joshua Chaplinsky, Stanley B. Webb, Jackk N. Killington, Kristen Callender, Michael Pollentine, Tony Rauch, Mark Cowling, and Alistair Rey.

Extremely Bizarre – A Bizarro/Extreme Horror Anthology

A lonely man gets more than he bargained for after ordering a hand-in-a-can from an old magazine.

Enter a world where face pareidolia is deadly and one mistake can lead to a horrifying death.

Join a traumatized woman as she returns to the place of her son's death, looking for something to fill the hole in her life.

Extremely Bizarre is an exquisite collection of ten tales accompanied by detailed illustrations.
Expect extreme horror. Expect bizarro. Expect therapy.

Trigger warnings: All of them.

Featuring tales by: Robert Guffey, Shaun Avery, Sergi G. Oset, Kevin J. Kennedy, Irene Ferraro-Sives, Cliff Mc-Nish, B. Patrick Lonberg, Todd Love, Melanie Atkinson, and Gerard Houarner.

Sons of Sorrow
by Matthew A. Clarke
SOME THINGS ARE BETTER LEFT ALONE

Henk has been living a relatively carefree life in the city since fleeing the horrors of the town of Sorrow with his

brother, Dave. Never would he have dreamt of returning.
Not even for her.

But time and banality have a funny way of eroding the
memory of even the worst experiences, bringing only
the better times to the forefront of recall, so when he
receives a wedding invitation from the third part of their
old monster-fighting trio, he finds himself unable to turn
it down.

Sorrow has changed drastically from the place it once
was, with the murders and suicides that once plagued
the town being used as a selling point by wealthy in-
vestors to turn it into a morbid attraction for dark
tourists.

Beneath the costumed mascots and smiling families, is
all really as it seems? Or by returning, have Henk and
Dave inadvertently awoken an ancient evil far deadlier
than anything they've faced before?

Sons of Sorrow is the latest bizarre horror from the mind
of Matthew A. Clarke.

Porn Land
By Kevin Shamel

OH, NO, PORN IS ILLEGAL!

That's right. Porn stars are criminals, pornographic web-
sites are being systematically destroyed, and not even
softcore or selfies are okay. And that's just in our world.
It's literally destroying the magick city of sexual expression—PORN LAND!

Phil and Zed, arriving through magickal means and
ill-equipped for adventure, must travel through the
erotic metropolis and gather pieces of THE PORNOMI-
CRON—a sexual spell-book that bridges our worlds.

And it won't be easy. They'll have to get past a giant
geisha and her samurai army, a determined detective
who's after their asses, a badass dominatrix and her gang,

a bunch more sexy people, a bunch of unsexy people...
And even more things that will freak you out and make
you horny—like a sperm monster and ambulance sex.
Will Phil and Zed put the book together, save Porn Land
and their new friends, *and* make pornography legal in
our world again? (Yes. It'd be a stupid story if they didn't.
But it's *how* they do it that you'll want to read about.)

It's a story about sucking, *and* not sucking. It's got
hardcore sex *and* a hardcore message. It's ridiculous
and you'll wanna rub one out to it. It's freakin' PORN
LAND, BABY!

Weird Fauna of the Multiverse
A trio of novellas by Leo X. Robertson
— A gimp becomes mesmerized by the koala at a zoo
on Venus. She draws him into the battle between the
purebred animal supremacy of the park's hippo owner
and the anti-establishmentarian koala uprising.
— In a godless future, a rich Martian traveler hunts the
former Vatican—now a hotspot for sex tourism—for his
deceased wife. When he discovers a dead priest in the
streets, he begins to investigate the weird plot of the
city's head cyberpope.
— Supercats spend their days responding to rescue calls
across their city. Since there aren't enough rescues to go
around, one supercat decides to do something drastic
and devious to resolve this crisis, changing the industry
forever.
The stories of *Weird Fauna of the Multiverse* explore
what happens to love and work when pushed beyond
the boundaries of human decency.

A Quaint New England Town
by Gregory L. Norris

When Ezra Wilson took the job as a census worker, he never imagined it would lead to a place like his latest assignment. From the moment he turns off the interstate and travels past the village limits, it becomes clear that Heritage isn't just some quaint New England town.

A sinister encounter at an automobile graveyard is only the start. In Heritage Proper, a town divided down the middle both politically and literally, Ezra is met with hostility on both sides of an imposing brick wall that separates warring factions that have maintained a fragile peace. After scaling the wall into Heritage North, Ezra discovers a beautiful young woman held prisoner in a fortified basement room and promises to help her. To do so will expose the last of the small town's dark secrets and lay bare big planetary dangers if Ezra survives his visit to a destination where even the white picket fences are not at all what they appear to be.

Russells in Time
by Kevin Shamel
Because you can never have enough Shamel! In this novella, a trio of recognizable characters find themselves travelling back in time and in the middle of a heated battle between the dinosaurs and a race of giant land-squid. Who will they side with? And will we get to see Russell Brand kicking ass in an Iron Man-esque suit? (Spoiler — yes. We totally will.)

Selleck's 'Stache is Missing!
by Charles Chadwick
Celebrated Hollywood star Tom Selleck has it all: talent, good looks, a winning personality, and a track record of television and movie hits, enjoyed by millions around

the world. Until one day, while filming his latest project, an old rival attacks him and steals his mustache. Now, lost and adrift, Tom struggles with his new life. Along with a group of dedicated crew members, celebrity friends, government agents, and the robot voice of an old co-star, he has to find the strength to take on his greatest role ever: tracking down his old rival, retrieving his legacy, and saving the world.

Songs About My Father's Crotch
by Dustin Reade

My father's crotch sang many songs, and the first of them all, was me.
Now it is my turn to sing, and I will sing to you of many things.
Here are my stories. Here are my songs.
I will sing of a man who wrestles furniture, and of a sister who disappears.
I will sing of modern day cannibalism, and Dwayne Johnson's elbow.
I will sing of foul-mouthed butterflies and plastic sharks, and I will hum a few bars about cartoon trains.
I will warble on about beards, sentient houses, monsters and Roald Dahl.
But mostly, with this collection of short stories, I will sing songs about my father's crotch.
Bizarro outsider, Dustin Reade, presents eleven stories of weirdo lit, culled from the deepest recesses of the human imagination, and sprinkled with thoughts and flakes from other parts of the body as well.
Don't miss it. Or do. Whatever.

The Secret Sex Lives of Ghosts
by Dustin Reade

Thomas Johansson can see ghosts after a near death experience, and has made a living killing them for a second time. After discovering that being possessed by a ghost causes an intense hallucinogenic effect, he goes into business with a perverted dead man named Jerry, selling possession as a street drug (street name: Ghost). But is the farmhouse he sees while possessed really a hallucination? Or is it something else?

The Falling Crystal Palace
by Carl Fuerst

The residents of Sterling, Indiana don't know who they are.

Sixty-one year old Tory Stebbins runs an Identity Verification agency that can help. But, as her town implodes, so does her business. She has fewer clients, stiffer competition, and her methods have become mysteriously ineffective. Most alarmingly, she's now suffering from the same problems she's helped her clients with over the length of her career.

Just when her situation seems beyond hope, Tory receives a cryptic message from Hoppy Bashford, her best friend who, forty years earlier, disappeared. "I don't want to say it's a life or death situation," writes Hoppy, "but I want to say it's a life or death situation."

Tory's quest to find Hoppy leads her through the strange, shifting landscapes of Sterling, and the enigmatic quarry around which it is built, and ultimately to the Crystal Palace Resort, a hotel and waterpark with an infinite maze of hallways, rooms, and bizarrely themed attractions whose size and scope defy physics and reason.

To locate her lost friend, escape from the resort, and find a cure for the identity-scrambling, reality-bending condition from which everyone in her world suffers, Tory must come to terms with who she is; she must de-

termine her place in, relationship to, and path through
the universe.

Dead Monkey Rum
by Robert Guffey

A mixture of urban fantasy and Los Angeles noir, *Dead
Monkey Rum* revolves around a stolen Tiki idol that
contains the ashes of visionary artist Stanislaw Szukals-
ki. Our heroes, an alcoholic monkey named Robert
McLintock and a beautiful bartender named Stephanie
Waterfall, must locate the missing statue in the wilds
of Los Angeles before a tribe of pissed-off Yetis can get
their massive, dirty paws on it. Because the obsidian
idol possesses magical properties, the Yetis want to use
it to kickstart the destruction of the human race, thus
paving the way for the cryptozoological beasts to take
humanity's place as the rulers of Earth.

Ebola Saves the Planet! and Other Wholesome Tales
by Matthew A. Clarke

A man gets a ticket to a popular gameshow and is willing
to risk life and limb to go home with the prize.

A family tries to survive in a world where gravity is
reversed and explosive balloon animals rule the streets.

A new epidemic hits the world. People are spontaneous-
ly erupting into mounds of steel coils, but after years, the
kids are growing restless. Will they be able to survive a
secret outing outside of their safehouse?

A young girl born to super villains feels out of place
among her family and peers. Upon discovering a das-
tardly plot to cause widespread catastrophe, will she
defy her family and save the planet?

106

Ebola Saves the Planet! and Other Wholesome Tales is a collection of eleven wild tales (and illustrations) from the mind of Matthew A. Clarke.